Total War

Dodge Merrin

Paperback ISBN-13: 979-8-9909079-4-2

Cover design by Calley Dunnihoo

Content Warning: *This book contains depictions of science fiction themed violence.*

Contents

Chapter One
Escape

Jimlian
Friday, March 5th, 2709
3:41 A.M.

Was that thunder?

The sound that reverberated through the complex had partially woken Leon from his slumber, but his sleep fogged mind seemed incapable of identifying its source.

Then it happened again, and his eyes shot wide open as he felt the unmistakable shuddering of a nearby explosion.

He leapt to his feet, then ran to his cell door and pressed his ear against it to listen for any clue as to what was happening.

The prison couldn't possibly be under attack, not this deep in Ordonian territory. Dare he hope someone had come to rescue him?

The hurried footsteps of several people approached his door, so he backed away to stand in the middle of the room and wait.

When the cell door flew open, several armored guards swarmed in with a Star Knight close behind. One guard ordered Leon to stand against the far wall, and he complied, backing up until he bumped the wall and raising his hands to signify he wasn't going to resist.

"What's going on?" he questioned as the knight closed the door.

"Quiet!" the knight hissed. He stood near the door, apparently listening for any threats approaching from the other side.

Even from his position on the other side of the room, Leon could hear shouting and several people running past. The Ordonians had placed him in a room in the center of the prison as an extra security measure, so there was no window through which to hear anything outside.

"I demand to know what is going on!" he insisted, only to receive a rifle butt to the abdomen.

Despite being a prisoner for over two weeks now, this was the first time anyone had hit him, not counting his initial capture, so he took the hint and waited quietly for whatever happened next.

He'd been treated well by the empire as the confederacy's president, despite its claims about not recognizing their legitimacy.

His cell was a relatively large room complete with a full-size bed, a desk, and a separate bathroom. They'd fed him three times a day, and this respectful treatment had continued even after he refused to answer any of their questions.

This could only mean they still didn't consider the Galactic Confederacy a true threat, or they would be using more persuasive methods in the effort to extract information.

The knight tensed, backed up as he drew his pistol, then aimed it at the door. Four of the five guards followed his lead, while the last one kept his weapon trained on Leon.

A firefight erupted outside the sealed door, and screams soon joined the sound of gunfire along with the reek of burnt flesh. Each of the guards gripped his weapon tighter, but the knight didn't react at all.

Then it grew quiet again.

The silence hung heavy on those ignorant of the fight's outcome, and one guard moved towards the door as if to check outside, but the knight signaled him to stay back.

Someone pounded on the door, causing everyone but the knight to nearly jump out of their skin.

"President Tyquese, this is Captain Turley. Please respond," a voice called.

The knight glared at Leon to warn him not to say anything, then responded in his stead.

"Prisoner, you have made a fatal mistake. Return to your cell immediately, and we might forego your execution."

"Ah, Knight Wensia. Thank you for confirming we have the right room."

The knight looked startled at the fact the captain knew his name, and his voice, but he recovered quickly enough to issue another threat.

"If you attempt to come through this door, we will kill our prisoner!"

No response.

Sparks and flames shot out from the door frame as someone used a cutter to sever the hinges and latch. It would be only a matter of seconds before they got through, leaving Wensia with little time to follow through on his threat.

The knight turned his gun on Leon, and there was no doubt in the president's mind that he would fire.

He grabbed the rifle of the guard covering him and pulled back, moving him into the line of fire just as Wensia pulled the trigger.

The guard relaxed his grip and Leon took the rifle for himself before diving to the floor just as the door was breached.

Several shots rang out, then there was silence.

When he looked up, Leon saw Captain Turley in a brown prison jumpsuit already reaching out to him.

"I thought you were still undercover with Zenzal's mercenaries," he commented as he took the offered hand.

"Your brother recalled me after you were stupid enough to trust an imperial and get yourself captured. You're welcome by the way," Turley responded.

"Mayor Kendrick isn't an imperial," Leon argued as he glanced around the room. All of the guards were dead, as was Wensia.

"I think he's proven otherwise."

"It would appear so," Leon admitted.

He looked towards the door where he spotted the lifeless body of a prisoner in the doorway with two more bodies in the corridor behind it. The price of his freedom.

"Let's get out of here," he urged, then followed Turley as he led the way through the complex.

Ten other prisoners joined them, but any others they came across ignored them in favor of tearing the place apart.

"Bit of a risk, freeing prisoners not under your command," Leon commented.

"Yes, but it was necessary. There was no way to smuggle enough of our people in here to overcome the guards. This way, the prison staff will be too preoccupied with the riot to worry about us," Turley responded.

True enough, the prison population was in full-scale riot, allowing their group to traverse the distance to the garages unchallenged.

They entered the main garage, finding it empty.

Or so they thought.

Upon passing a carbocrete column, a thin object swung around from the other side and connected with Leon's face.

There was the sensation of falling backward, then his world went dark.

GCS Runner
6:01 A.M.

"What happened?" General Sam Tyquese asked when he saw the grim expression of the lieutenant approaching him.

He'd worked through the night, but he didn't feel sleepy in the slightest thanks to his anxiety regarding the rescue attempt of his brother, both anxiety and sleeplessness fueled by the steaming cup of coffee on the desk beside him.

Captain Turley was a capable man, but Leon was being held on Jimlian, an Ordonian stronghold planet. Should they manage to make it out of the prison, there was still a large garrison for them to contend with.

With circumstances like that, it was easy for things to go wrong, and the look on the lieutenant's face seemed to indicate they had.

"Captain Turley reported in. They managed to get off the planet, but the president was injured during the escape."

"How bad?"

"Unknown. The message didn't include any details."

That was to be expected since a longer message increased the likelihood of it getting intercepted and traced.

Sam dismissed the lieutenant and returned to his work.

There was no point worrying about it now. He'd find out exactly what happened and how bad it was later.

Vehla
United
6:11 A.M.

The early hour found Primary Max Canza working in his governor's office, earnestly seeking to maintain control over their recent gains.

The confederacy's emergence and initial victory posed a large threat within the Vehlan territories. Mayor Kendrick and some others had proven their loyalty when they assisted in the capture of Leon Tyquese, but he couldn't take the risk others would see this as an opportunity to rebel.

"Enter," he said in response to a knock on his door. A lieutenant came in, approached the desk, and stood at attention to deliver his report.

"The enemy leader has escaped, sir."

"Explain."

"There was a riot in the prison, and order hasn't yet been fully restored, but it was determined that several pirates managed to escape along with Tyquese. Jimlian's governor has already grounded all outbound flights, but requires your authorization to recall those that left shortly after the riot began."

"Authorization granted. Ground all flights on Hrion and Pekata until further notice as well. Dismissed."

He closed out the Vehlan territorial security reports displayed on his desk and brought up a tactical view of the core nations in its place.

An attempt by the confederacy to rescue its president came as no surprise, but he found their level of success disturbing.

Jimlian was deep in imperial territory where it was safe from a full-scale attack, leaving a surgical strike as the only possibility of freeing Tyquese. The best strategy was to infiltrate the prison and break him out from the inside, but they shouldn't have been able to do that so far from their support base.

Two Star Knights had also been assigned to guard the man in twelve hour shifts, so any escape or rescue attempt should have failed immediately, yet several prisoners had managed to get out.

The confederacy was apparently much stronger than any of them had speculated. They had come out of nowhere to win the first battle, killing Secondary Farra in the process, then proceeded to destroy Zenzal's mercenary base by smuggling a nuclear weapon inside.

It was possible the Nosine rebellion was their doing as well, a theory supported by reports of former slaves fighting alongside Vehlan soldiers in the few ground engagements of the war to date.

Now they had effected a successful escape from a maximum security prison deep within Ordonian territory.

If this trend continued, the empire was looking at more nations moving against it, not to mention further rebellions.

They needed a win, and soon.

7:42 A.M.

A nasty headache greeted Leon as he woke, so he kept his eyes shut and debated if he really did have to go to work today.

The pain subsided a little, and then he remembered what had already transpired that morning and slowly opened his eyes, fearing the worst. He breathed a short sigh of relief when he saw Captain Turley sitting in front of him with his back against a box and pistol on the floor next to him.

He sat up, then fell back against a box when a wave of dizziness struck him. When it passed, he looked around to discover they were in a cargo hold with the troopers comprising his rescue party either standing around or sitting on boxes, all of them still in the brown jumpsuits worn by Ordonian prisoners.

"About time you woke up," Turley commented.

"How long was I out?"

"Over four hours. A prison guard hit you in the face with a rifle, knocking you out and forcing us to drag you the rest of the way."

"Where are we?"

"A cargo transport."

"Imperial?"

"We've worked with this crew before. They won't betray us. We'll be rendezvousing with one of our gunships soon," the captain explained.

"Turley, you'd better get up here," a voice suggested over the intercom.

The captain grabbed his pistol and holstered it as he stood up, then left in the direction of the bridge. Leon followed, steadying himself against boxes and walls as his balance slowly returned.

"What is it?" Turley questioned.

"There's a light cruiser bearing down on us, demanding we follow them back to Jimlian," the pilot responded.

"What did you tell them?" Leon asked.

"I reported we have perishable cargo that must be delivered on schedule."

"Did they believe you?"

"Negative. They're now demanding we drop out of hyperspace and prepare to be boarded."

"That escalated fast."

"Imperial citizens normally follow orders immediately and without question. Only criminals make excuses to do otherwise," the pilot explained, then dropped the ship out of hyperspace.

"What are you doing?"

"We can't outfight or outrun them, and I'm not willing to sacrifice my ship and crew for you."

"He's right. Our best chance lies in overpowering the boarding party, then taking their transport back to the cruiser and commandeering it," Turley suggested.

"Then I guess we're fighting. I need a weapon," Leon responded.

"We have some stashed in the hold."

"Wait! We have another contact! They're firing!"

They looked at the main screen in time to see a pair of rockets strike the cruiser, followed closely by a shot from a laser cannon.

The attack did little damage, and the Ordonians turned to face their attacker. More shots hit them, but now the cruiser was returning fire.

"Does this ship have any weapons?" Leon asked.

"Not anything that can hurt a warship."

"Fire on them anyway. Our combined firepower may be enough to collapse their shields."

The pilot hesitated, but then Turley repeated the order while tapping his fingers on the pistol still holstered at his hip. He got the message, and opened fire with the transport's laser guns.

This caused the cruiser to fire on them as well as the newcomer, but the divided firepower was weaker and inflicted little damage.

The cruiser's shields collapsed within minutes, and it was drifting harmlessly soon after.

"We're being hailed," the pilot reported.

"Put it through."

"This is GCS Cascade to Captain Turley. Are you receiving?"

"I am. What are you doing here?"

"We intercepted a transmission from Jimlian ordering all ships launched within the past four hours to be intercepted and escorted back. We weren't sure you'd make it to the rendezvous, so we decided to come find you."

"Good thinking, Trooper. What's your status?" Leon chimed in.

"Minor damage. We're good to go, sir."

"Send over a shuttle," Turley ordered before he cut the connection.

"Mr. President, please return to the others and prepare to disembark. I'll join you shortly," Turley requested. Leon guessed what he was about to do and left the bridge without another word.

"What I am about to do keeps you out of jail," he heard Turley say before he was out of earshot.

GCS Runner
8:01 A.M.

"Whoa! What happened to your face?" Sam commented. Even through a video screen, his brother's face looked like it had slammed into a brick wall.

"I discovered why it's a good idea to have a helmet in battle. What's our status?" Leon answered the question before moving on to more important matters.

"The Ordonians are still consolidating their forces while at the same time trying to learn more about us. I get the feeling they still don't know for sure what nations comprise the confederacy," Sam began.

"That was the information they were trying the hardest to get out of me, so that tracks, but what do you mean 'you get the feeling'? I thought you had sources within the imperial government?"

"I do, but the emperor has greatly restricted information since the first battle. Not even Captain Turley's sources go that deep."

"Alright, continue."

"We managed to disrupt Ordonian patrols on the former Vehlan border by destroying their primary base on Raxin, but nobody took advantage of the situation. The majority of the population within the Vehlan territories still appears content with imperial rule," Sam reported.

"I was hoping the emergence of the confederacy would change their minds, but I wasn't counting on it. It's enough to keep the enemy off-balance for now. What about the attack on Acker and his pirates?"

"Their main base was totally destroyed, cutting their numbers by nearly a quarter. Zenzal is in the process of making them a mobile force to safeguard their remaining numbers, but so far they've been quiet."

"Anything else?"

"Yes. I received word that our new ships are ready for service. There are still a few things to be done, but they have been thoroughly tested and the engineers are confident they are ready for service. Everything that's left can be taken care of by the crews after launch."

"When are they set to be commissioned?"

"The project leaders are waiting for us to give final approval. I ordered the captain of your ship to take you to the shipyard, and I'm on the way as well," Sam concluded.

"Good. I'll see you there."

Chapter Two
Leveling The Playing Field

Terakin
Tuesday, March 9th, 2709
9:53 A.M.

"There they are at last," Leon whispered to himself.

Four large ships surrounded on five sides by skeletal construction docks greeted the president's transport as it entered orbit above the fifth planet in the Atrias system, their profiles barely visible through the framework.

Two were a three hull design with the outer hulls connected to the center by large struts and significantly smaller than the central section, making them look almost like wings. The main hull was rectangular save for the front where the sides angled inward to create a pointed bow.

The other two had a circular section in the middle with a flat top and bottom while the front was triangular and the back a symmetrical trapezoid.

These were the first of the confederacy's new dreadnaught and carrier classes. Leon was headed to one of the dreadnaughts where he would meet up with Sam for a tour, and he couldn't wait to learn everything about them.

He'd seen the initial designs and was kept updated during the entire building process, but none of that compared to being able to see the finished product in person.

His transport finally docked and Leon walked off the side ramp to find Sam already waiting for him.

"You're looking better or, at least normal," his brother commented.

"Hard work comes with a price."

"Is that supposed to make me want to work harder?"

"President Tyquese, General Tyquese, welcome aboard," a familiar voice spoke up. Leon followed it to its source to see Captain William Dex, the Vehlan overseer of the project, walking towards them with a woman at his side.

"Thank you, Captain. It's good to be here," Leon responded, accepting the captain's hand and shaking it.

"Glad to see you safely out of imperial hands," he commented, then added, "This is Dr. Pera Naton, the Vaton overseer of the project."

"Pleasure to meet you," Leon said as he reached out his hand.

"Same here. I've enjoyed working on this project and am proud to work with Vehlans again," Naton responded, accepting the hand.

"We're anxious to see what you've done here. Let's get started."

"Of course. Follow us," Dex prompted, then led the way off the hangar deck.

"The first thing I'd like to know is, how did you get these ships built so quickly? Building something on this scale, at least as far as prototypes are concerned, should have taken years," Sam questioned.

"When it comes to a single nation working on it, you're absolutely right. Resources have to be budgeted, increasing build time and often resulting in discontinuation of the project, but this time we have the resources of several nations behind us, reducing the strain on each one and speeding construction," Naton replied.

"Exactly. The Merchant's Interest provided the funding, the Amberlis Territories provided the materials, and Atrias took care of the labor.

This helped to shield the project from imperial intelligence as well," Dex added.

"All of that may have helped, but I still have trouble believing this is already done. It's barely been a year since you started, and that's including the design phase!"

"We almost had a dreadnaught design finished before the Ordonians invaded Vehla and Colonel Tyquese had the foresight to hide copies of those designs on other planets before the empire completely cut us off. The carriers we had to start from scratch, but knowing your home is in the hands of conquerors is a great motivator to work faster," Dex explained.

"The capture of the Secret Fire by your pirates also provided a boost, in more ways than one. First, it provided the insights we needed to finalize our designs. Second, we stripped it of parts and used them in the construction," Naton added.

"What parts did you use?" Leon asked.

"The weapons we upgraded and installed on one dreadnaught and used the power cores on the other."

They kept walking as they talked, skirting workers and equipment as needed. The primary systems were all online, but there was still plenty of activity as less important systems were finished and wall plating was installed.

"Okay, that explains the dreadnaughts. What about the carriers?" Sam pressed.

"My destroyer was part of a carrier group when it was ambushed in the last year of the war. They targeted the carrier first and managed to disable it, but most of the rest of us were able to break through their lines and escape. When I was brought onto this project, I sent a salvage crew out to the carrier. The computer core was still good, so we reprogrammed it and installed it on one carrier. Anything else that was salvageable was used on the other one," Dex explained.

"Alright, enough about how quickly the ships were built. Why don't you give us some actual specs?" Leon suggested.

"Gladly. Both ships are equipped with plasma weapons, matching their firepower to that of the Ordonians," Dex began.

"The dreadnaughts also have the enhanced railguns. This may seem like antiquated technology to the casual observer, but these weapons were recently developed by Vaton engineers. They are capable of bypassing a ship's shields and impacting its hull directly, inflicting significant damage," Naton continued.

"How?"

"The specifics are included in the data packets we sent both of you, but basically the weapons use a combination of both projectile and energy based weaponry that current shield technology is not designed to protect against. Even our own engineers are still working on a viable defense."

"At least that means the empire won't be able to steal the shielding. Let's hope they don't steal the weapon," Sam observed.

"What's next?" Leon prodded.

"That would be the layered shielding. This technology has been known for quite some time, but implementation was slow due to extreme power requirements. The union actually developed a method a couple years ago, but was unable to make use of it," Dex chimed in.

"I remember," Leon commented, then elaborated for Sam's benefit. "The design was too complex to upgrade existing ships, and the power systems had to be redesigned for each class before it could be included on new ones, but we ran out of time before we could start producing the new ships. It was too late to win the war for the union, but it can still help win the war for the confederacy."

"So you are talking about two layers of combat shields on top of the basic shielding, right?" Sam checked for clarification.

"Correct."

"Alright, what else is there?"

“That's it for the dreadnaughts. The carriers also have plasma weaponry and layered shielding, but in their case, the extra shielding is only around the hangar bays to conserve power for the launch systems.”

“No railguns?”

“No railguns. As of right now, the railguns are too large to move independently of the ship. Since carriers are not technically combat vessels, it was decided they would have little chance to use them and the power was better utilized elsewhere.”

“Is that all?” Leon questioned, the disappointment plain in his voice.

“No. The most significant improvement is in the fighter launch bays. These ships can launch their second wave almost immediately after the first, granting you double the number of fighters your enemy can field in the same amount of time,” Naton reassured him.

They finally reached the bridge, and the project leaders fell silent to give the president and general a chance to look around.

While the rest of the ship was still hard at work on the last stages of construction, here all was quiet. The bridge crew stood at their stations in full dress uniform, the bright white of the few Vatons standing out in sharp contrast to the dark blue of the Vehlan majority.

Leon surveyed the bridge from the entrance situated between the tactical and operations stations. From there it was a straight shot to the captain's chair in the middle and a few feet in front of that sat Helm and Navigation.

When he had taken it all in, he casually walked up to and around the captain's chair to take a seat.

“The only thing they need right now are names,” Sam said from behind him.

“Their names will reflect the goals and ideals of this new confederacy, as will those that follow them. The dreadnaughts will be known as Victory and Justice and the carriers shall bear the names of Freedom and Independence,” Leon responded, eliciting a round of applause from the crew.

A lieutenant ran up to Sam, whispered something in his ear, then rushed off again as the general activated his palco to view a new report.

"Looks like the empire is finally over its initial surprise. Zenzal's mercenaries just conducted two raids against the Amberlis Territories, and a fleet is mobilizing in the Merchant's Interest," he reported.

"Then it's time we got moving as well. Send a trooper squadron to the territories to assist the local defense forces, then you take all four of these new ships at the head of a fleet and deal with the threat within the interest," Leon ordered.

"You're not going to lead the battle yourself?"

"No. Right now I need to finish organizing our forces and planning our campaign. After that, it's on to recruiting more nations to our cause," Leon replied.

Standing, he gestured towards the captain's chair and said, "For now, the fighting is up to you."

Chapter Three
It Begins

Vehla
Wednesday, March 10th, 2709
8:48 P.M.

The sun had set long ago, but the darkness that came with its passing was little different than the light of midday to the woman hiding in the doorway of a bombed out store. She could use specialized lenses to allow her native Ordonian eyes to see clearly in the dim light of the blue sun, but Wendy Ricine preferred to rely on her instincts rather than technological crutches.

Dirt and grease covered every inch of her, leaving her skin barely visible and darkening her blonde hair while her clothes were a pair of torn pants, an old long-sleeved shirt, and frayed athletic shoes, but her green eyes were as sharp as ever as she watched the ruined street before her with laser intensity.

Reconstruction of the Vehlan capital was nearly complete, but that effort had yet to reach this place. The town of Montlion was less than an hour away from the capital when traveling by ground vehicle, and this had led to it suffering heavily during the bombardment of the planet. Since Governor Canza was putting most of his effort into restoring the capital beyond its former glory, towns like this continued to lay in ruins, inhabited primarily by scavengers and criminals.

She spotted someone coming towards her and locked her gaze upon him, then took two steps out of the doorway upon recognizing him.

"What have you found out?" she questioned.

The man, who sported an appearance similar to her own, stopped a few feet away and slowly looked around them before responding. She did not know his name, nor did he know hers.

"I successfully infiltrated the governor's residence as a low-level aide. I've talked to many of the staff, and looked everywhere I could. I couldn't find any evidence of disloyalty on the part of the governor," he reported.

"There are no signs he's assembling his staff with people loyal to him first and the emperor second?"

"None. Everyone I talked to declared their absolute loyalty to the empire, and there is nothing in their files to suggest otherwise."

"What about the new armor? Did you learn the location of the production factory?"

"Negative. It appears the only people who know that are the adjutant governor and Canza himself."

"Is there anything else to report?" she asked, and he shook his head no.

"Where do you want me to look next?"

"Nowhere. The emperor has suspended my investigation, so you are not to conduct any more active inquiries. You are to maintain your current position and await further instructions. The knights are not yet convinced of his loyalty and we may wish to resume our examination at a later date," she replied, then dismissed him with a wave of her hand.

All this time investigating Canza, and she had yet to find a single shred of evidence to indict him in a conspiracy against the emperor. All indications were that he was the most loyal man she'd ever met.

She continued to brood on this as she left her spot and walked down the street until she was stopped by someone stepping out in front of her.

"Stand aside," she demanded. She sensed two others approaching behind her and tensed for a fight, but remained calm and did not strike out.

"Not until you tell me what you're doing here," the man blocking her path responded, nearly choking her with his rancid breath. His clothes hung off him in strips, his shoes were held together with string, and he clearly hadn't bathed in weeks.

"I'm just trying to survive, same as you," she told him, causing his eyes to narrow in anger.

"I'm not stupid. You're obviously an Ordonian. There's no reason for you to be here."

"I disagree," Ricine commented.

"With what?"

"You *are* stupid."

The man yelled with rage and swung a fist at her, but she blocked it with one hand and throat punched him with the other.

She then ducked and spun around with her right foot out in front of her, tripping one of the men behind her before using her remaining momentum to drive a fist into the other one's gut. After that she resumed a standing position and quickly delivered successive kicks to both their jaws, rendering them unconscious.

When she turned to face the one who had confronted her, she found him staring wide-eyed at his friends on the ground.

"You have shown yourself to be lacking in intelligence, as well as a troublemaker. This world will be improved by your absence," she commented as she drew a knife.

The man's eyes locked on the blade, widened even further, then he turned and ran.

She threw the knife, scoring a hit when it embedded itself in the back of his thigh to send him sprawling onto the ground. She then casually walked up to him, retrieved her knife, and flipped him onto his back.

"Please don't kill me!"

"You brought this on yourself," she responded, then stabbed him in the chest.

Vehla
Thursday, March 11th, 2709
10:23 A.M.

The city stretched out before Canza, thrumming with activity as construction efforts continued amid the sparkling spires which were already completed.

It was only a year later, but the city of United was already unrecognizable. All of the destruction wrought by the nuclear device was gone as was the siege base that once stood amid the ruins. It wouldn't be long before there wasn't a single mark of war left to be found.

All new structures, such as the governor's residence he now occupied, were getting built according to Ordonian designs. Many of these already dotted the city, and more were under construction. The lights were the dark blue preferred by the natives, but that was the only difference from structures found on any other imperial planet.

Meanwhile, in an effort to appease the Vehlans, he'd ordered any salvageable buildings that had survived the blast to be accurately restored. Most of these were on the outer edges, so a distinct line was starting to appear between the Ordonian and Vehlan.

He'd have to find a way to correct that. They were supposed to be eliminating the lines, not building new ones.

Surprisingly, the Vehlans weren't resisting in any way. In fact, most of them were throwing themselves into the work. He initially suspected this was merely a ploy and restricted them from doing too much, but now he was thinking their attitude was genuine and was granting them more and more responsibility. He was even allowing them to join local security forces, freeing up the imperial troops for use elsewhere.

Some of this was due to the fact Kendrick had delivered on his offer to ambush Tyquese and turn him over. Many of those that participated in his plan were Vehlan, and not one of them had tried to thwart it.

"Governor?" an aide said from behind him.

"What is it?"

"We've detected an enemy fleet on its way to the Merchant's Interest. They're on a direct course for the fleet we are assembling in that sector."

"Get a comlink to Knight Ricine, then prep the Lentaise Three for immediate departure and get me a shuttle," Canza ordered, finally leaving the balcony and returning to his desk as the aide left the room.

"What is it?" Ricine asked once the connection was made. She had chosen to accept it as audio only.

"I want you to send the legionnaires to the border of the Vaton Conglomerate to scout out the situation there, then you are to join me in the Merchant's Interest."

"You want me to leave the legion alone?"

"It's time they started learning some independence, and they won't be in any danger for the time being."

"Confirmed," Ricine responded, then signed off.

Both of them knew the real reason Canza wanted her to join him was so he could keep a closer eye on her, and it was because she wanted to watch him that she had accepted so readily.

The primary leaned back in his chair and laughed softly, amused at how much like politicians the two of them were behaving. The job of a soldier was to destroy the enemy, not to engage in political scheming.

Temporarily transferring his powers on this planet to the adjutant governor, he finally left for his shuttle. It was time to show those anarchists in the confederacy the power of the empire.

GCS Victory
Monday, March 15th, 2709
6:53 P.M.

The main screen showed nothing but the blank whiteness of hyperspace, but General Sam Tyquese stared at it as if his life depended on it. They were only minutes away from engaging the Ordonians in the first real battle of this war, a fight with which he had sworn to never again get involved.

The war he left behind was over, but this one was just beginning.

This one was going to be different.

At least, that's what he kept telling himself.

"Approaching target coordinates, sir," Helm reported.

They were as ready as they were ever going to be, so he gave the order to drop to normal space, the ship's combat systems automatically going to full power the moment they did so.

"Ordonian fleet ahead, sir. They outnumber us by fifty percent."

"Commence attack."

Every ship in the confederate fleet quickly complied and launched a volley of plasma, laser, and missiles at the imperials. The fighters were kept on defense for now, and neither of the dreadnaughts used their railguns but instead stayed in the center of the fleet as if for protection.

The opposing fleet's interceptors stopped most of what came at them while the rest was easily deflected by shields.

Blue glows flared out from behind the Ordonian ships as they accelerated towards the confederates, returning fire and spreading out as they traversed the space between them.

"Move up," Sam calmly ordered, and the confederates pushed forward. Unlike the enemy, he kept his ships grouped together to maximize firepower.

For the first several minutes, each side held its own, but then the Ordonians began gaining the advantage. Sam allowed this to continue for a few minutes, long enough to let his opponents think they were winning. When enough time had passed, he gave Tactical a pre-arranged hand signal.

The ships in the center of the confederate front line spread apart, allowing the two dreadnaughts to take their place.

Then the Ordonians pulled most of their ships back to the center, clearing the way for their own dreadnaughts to charge forward, the flagship class leading the way.

A sly smile spread across Sam's face as the overconfident Ordonians reacted exactly the way he and his brother had predicted. If only he could see their faces after what came next.

"Second wave, commence attack," he ordered.

Several confederate destroyers, along with their escorts, dropped out of hyperspace all around the enemy fleet.

"Target railguns on enemy command ship. Fire when ready."

OES Lentaise Three
7:22 P.M.

"Perimeter ships, refocus on enemy reinforcements!" Primary Canza ordered. Knight Ricine showed no reaction to the new enemy ships, nor to the primary's response, but merely continued to observe from her position standing to his left.

Violent tremors rocked the ship, sparks flew from consoles, and crew members jerked away from their stations as if they had become live bombs.

An awkward silence descended on the bridge as Canza looked around to see many of the crew projecting the same disbelief he felt himself.

That had felt like a direct hit on the hull, but that was impossible. Their shields were still fully operational.

"What happened?" he asked.

"A weapon went right through our shields and struck a direct hit! Moderate damage!"

More shaking from a similar hit, and this time, systems went off-line.

Needing to see for himself, Canza leapt from his chair and ran to the tactical station. He was just in time to see one of the enemy dreadnaughts fire a beam of white light the likes of which he'd never seen before.

He gripped the console tight with one hand and kept his eyes on the display as the beam passed through both layers of shielding and struck the hull directly, causing significant damage.

"Evasive maneuvers! Target all weapons on that ship!" he ordered, pointing at the one that had just fired. He then gave the order for his escort ships to focus on the other enemy dreadnaught.

He was still at the tactical station when another shot from the enemy headed straight for the bridge, sending him diving for cover while he grabbed Ricine's arm and pulled her down at the same time.

The primary kept his head down and held on tight to Ricine as the deck bucked wildly beneath them.

A support beam detached from the ceiling and landed inches to their right, but they were unharmed.

When it was over, Canza jumped up, skirted the beam which had fallen where Ricine was standing moments before and sat in the command chair.

There were some groans from crew members, but a quick glance told him they were all still alive.

"Heavy damage, sir! Multiple hull breaches, but shields are still at ninety-six percent!" Tactical reported, his voice shaking.

No new attacks came, so Canza took advantage of the lull to check the status of the battle at large on his command console where he saw that one of his destroyers had engaged the enemy dreadnaught.

One of his own dreadnaughts was destroyed and the other had suffered heavy damage while the fleet's perimeter ships were out of the fight and the interior ones were taking heavy fire.

For the first time in his life, he was unsure of what to do.

Another strike on the hull rocked the ship, bursting lights and nearly throwing him from his chair, but the restraints did their job and he remained seated.

"Sir, that last one severed the starboard arm!"

Another shot like that, and they were finished.

"All ships, retreat!"

The crew looked at him, shocked into inaction that he would give such an order.

"Follow your orders!" Ricine shouted, snapping them out of it.

The retreat order was sent out, and the fleet quickly jumped into hyperspace. Now that they were safe, Canza checked his display for the final results.

Less than half the fleet remained, the only ones undamaged enough to make the jump.

"They have a foothold now," Ricine commented.

"Yes."

That one small word was heavy with meaning understood by both of them.

This fleet was their main line of defense in the territory, and the planetary garrisons were not yet what they needed to be to withstand an attack.

He had effectively ceded the Merchant's Interest to the enemy.

GCS Victory
7:44 P.M.

The bridge crew erupted into cheers and applause as hyperspace entry flashes dotted the main screen, leaving empty space in place of the enemy ships.

They had done it! They had met the empire in full-out battle and won!

It was even better that they had forced them to retreat. An Ordonian fleet hadn't retreated from any battle for years!

"There's still a few enemy ships out there, sir," Sam's second reminded him.

"Send a signal telling them to surrender and prepare to be boarded. Pick up any escape pods you find, from either side, and see to it that everyone is properly taken care of. I'm going to go tell the president the news," Sam responded before leaving the bridge for the adjoining conference room.

Chapter Four
Shattered Pride

Vehlan Border Outpost
Wednesday, March 17th, 2709
9:03 A.M.

Primary Canza glared at the near wreck of the Lentaise Three from an observation deck overlooking the space station's repair bay. One of the most powerful ships the empire had ever built, and it fell to the onslaught of violent upstarts.

Here it sat, full of holes and largely inoperable after barely making it this far. A large chunk of it, the entire starboard arm, had been blasted off the ship and was still floating around the battle site. Simply despicable.

While traveling to this base, he had gone over the sensor logs from the battle and personally surveyed the damage. Despite the devastation to the rest of the ship, the shields had taken only minor damage. The shields surrounded the hull in a protective layer, two layers with the new shielding, so damaging the hull required first destroying that protection.

Shields were damaged and destroyed when the generators projecting them overloaded from power surges caused by weapon impacts. When enough failed, the entire shield went down.

None of this damage was to be found on the Lentaise Three, and none of the hits on the hull had impacted the generators. Clearly the confederates were making a point about the extent of their capabilities.

The readings the sensors had taken regarding the shots fired at them were unclear, leaving him with nothing more than speculations as to what it had been. To determine its exact nature, he had engineers going over every inch of the data as well as the damage to the ship. This was just as well since his brooding over the defeat was clouding his own engineer's mind.

He had allowed his pride to take over, causing him to get blindsided by the enemy. That was something he had vowed to never let happen, but now he had. So many others had been destroyed in the same manner, and he had always looked down on them, but now he was one of them.

"Primary Canza?" someone said from behind, snapping him out of his thoughts.

He turned to see a man in an engineer's uniform with commander's insignia facing him and displaying a report with his palco. The commander was a few inches shorter than him, but still carried himself with confidence in the presence of his superior.

"What have you learned?" Canza asked.

"We have determined the nature of the weapon that inflicted the damage upon the Lentaise Three, sir," the commander told him, and held the report up for him to see.

"I'll study the details later. Just give me the basics," Canza said with a wave of his hand.

"It was a railgun weapon, sir."

There was no way he'd heard that correctly.

"Are you telling me that my ship was nearly destroyed by an antique?"

"Not precisely, sir. The weapon was a railgun, but it is a new and more advanced design. We are still determining exactly how it functions."

"How was it able to penetrate our shields?" Canza questioned. As he was talking, he was also working the whole thing out in his own mind.

Reliable historical records only went back about five hundred years, and in the earliest of those records railgun weaponry was in use. Even then, they had been on their way out as energy shields became strong enough to render them almost useless. Eventually they were completely replaced by energy weaponry, which were capable of causing far more of a drain on shields.

None of this explained how any weapon, modern or otherwise, could penetrate energy shields, especially those of the advanced design on the Lentaise Three. Shields were capable of stopping everything until depleted, but against this weapon it was as if they didn't even exist.

"That's what we're still working on. Right now, all we have is a working theory, sir," the commander answered.

The primary's only response was to give the man an impatient look.

"We've ascertained from the sensor data that the weapon fires a solid projectile in much the same way as previous designs. However, this projectile is surrounded by an energy field, and we think the relationship between the two creates a previously unknown effect that shields were never designed to block. We're determining the exact nature of that effect now, sir."

"This is to be top-priority for all engineering departments. Figure this out and create a defense against it. This is not going to happen again," Canza firmly issued his orders. At this point Knight Ricine walked up to him, but he intentionally ignored her, dismissed the engineer, and looked back out the window. He wasn't in the mood to listen to her gloat.

"You have a call from the emperor," she said shortly, with a surprising tone of softness to her voice. The primary made sure he was fully composed, then made his way to the nearest conference room.

She followed behind him.

9:37 A.M.

"My emperor, I will invade the Vaton Conglomerate," Canza stated, calmly staring at the hologram of Emperor Lentaise in the center of the conference table.

For several minutes he hadn't said a word, patiently waiting for the monarch to vent his anger before answering the question of how he was going to prove his worthiness to continue as the empire's top military commander.

Knight Ricine was also present, but she had done nothing but stand beside the door and watch.

He had noticed she was good at standing silently and simply observing, but he wasn't quite sure if he felt that was a good thing or a bad thing. At least she wasn't always trying to tell him how to run his command.

"Explain," Lentaise prompted.

"Those railguns could only have come from the conglomerate and they are the enemy's biggest advantage right now. I will eliminate the source, after which our superior numbers and resources will allow us to control the situation."

"You couldn't stop the confederates in the Merchant's Interest, what makes you think you can defeat the Vatons?"

"Now that I know what we're up against, I can counter it."

"The reports I've seen say we won't have a viable defense against these railguns for at least several weeks, if not months."

"A technological advantage, especially a new one, only goes so far. Careful tactical planning can be used to counter it until a technological counter-advantage can be created."

"Are you planning on leaving the Merchant's Interest to the enemy?"

"Yes, I am. The forces we have there are capable of holding out for quite some time. By the time they are defeated the Interest will be of little use to the victors."

He didn't like the idea of ordering so many men and women to die fighting a battle he knew they couldn't win, but such sacrifices were necessary in any war.

The emperor appeared to calm down a little while he took a minute to weigh his options. He was perfectly capable of running this war himself, and was most likely considering doing exactly that.

"Take your legionnaires and attack the conglomerate as you suggest. I will begin developing my own strategies for victory while you focus on that invasion and work on a defense against the railguns. Knight Ricine, you are to continue acting as his executive officer," Lentaise finally ordered.

"Understood, your majesty," Canza and Ricine said at the same time. After that, the emperor disconnected and Canza turned to leave, but Ricine blocked his way.

"Why did you save my life?" she questioned.

"I had no reason to do otherwise."

"I'm a Star Knight, I've questioned your authority, and I've been reporting your every move to the emperor."

"Those aren't reasons for wanting you dead. I may not approve of your occupation or your actions, but wanting someone dead requires more than simple disapproval," Canza explained.

She continued to block the door as she considered that answer, and Canza waited patiently.

"Why did you choose me as your executive officer with the legionnaires?" she finally asked.

"We've already discussed this."

"You never gave me a satisfactory answer. I let it go at the time, but now I am demanding you tell me the whole truth," Ricine insisted. Admittedly enjoying this small diversion, the primary took a seat and gave her a subtle smile.

"Since you're so good at discerning why I wouldn't do something, why don't you give me some reasons why I wouldn't keep you with the legion," he challenged.

"I'm a Star Knight, and it is a well-known fact that regular military personnel despise and distrust the Star Knights. This is especially true of primaries, as a few have even tried to dissolve the order. There isn't anything that you can learn from me that could damage the knights, but allowing me near you puts you in a risky position."

"It's true that I don't like the Star Knights and I definitely don't trust them, but I have no desire to see them destroyed. They have their purpose within our society, and they serve it well. Every risk is a calculated one, including allowing you near me. I have nothing to hide, minimizing the risk to myself."

"That still doesn't answer my question."

"So far the reasons you have given me, for both questions, relate to the organization that you belong to. Has it occurred to you that my reasons might be on the level of the individual?" Canza asked. This time she didn't respond, only waited.

"There is something different about you than the other knights. You have accomplished a lot, you have the ambition to do even more, and you have no shortage of confidence, but you don't define yourself by these things. There is a rare quality to you that allows you to do what is necessary to thrive in this world while remaining your own person. It is this quality that has intrigued me, and it is this quality that I wish to investigate," he finally explained.

When Ricine still didn't say anything, he rose from his chair and stood in front of her. After a moment she stepped to the side, allowing him to leave the room.

Ordeos Prime
9:50 A.M.

The conversation with Canza having come to a satisfactory conclusion, Emperor Johan Lentaise turned to the books lining the shelves behind his desk. He found the one he wanted near the middle, pulled it out, then went to the large chair in the sitting area on the right side of his office and sat down.

Most information was stored electronically with intense security measures protecting sensitive material, but that written within these books was written by emperors, empresses, princes and princesses, or their aides, for use by royals only. For that, they chose not to trust even the most secure of anti-intrusion software.

This one was written by the fourth emperor, and Johan turned to the section written immediately following the Merchant's War fought against the Vehlan Union.

That war ended in disaster for the empire when the Vehlans deployed a new ship class outfitted with advanced defensive systems. A fleet of those ships managed to make its way almost single-handedly to a striking position against Ordeos Prime itself.

Finally admitting he had no means of stopping them, the emperor sued for peace, eventually being forced to turn over several star systems to the union. The passage now before Johan was that emperor's thoughts on how to prevent such a defeat in the future.

> *First and foremost, we must guarantee we are at the very forefront of technological and scientific advancement. This applies to every field of research, not only weapons technology as in the past. Our arrogance blinded us to advances in defensive systems, allowing our enemies to leap ahead in that regard. That mistake nearly destroyed us.*

One of the most powerful medicines ever discovered was found in mold, possibly the least likely place to look for such a thing. We must take this lesson to heart and apply it to all pursuits. Advantages over our enemies can also be found in the most unlikely of places.

Secondly, we must know our enemy. We assumed the fractured nature of the union to be its biggest weakness, but in this case, it was their biggest strength. The technical knowledge of the Vatons combined with the production capability of the Vehlans fueled by the resources of the Merchants created the ships that nearly destroyed us.

We must remember this strength in our enemies, as it can be turned to our advantage. They are strong together, but remove a single element from the equation, and the rest will fall.

Finally, when answers elude you, look to those who have gone before. The aliens are gone now, but pieces of their legacy still remain. To this day, we have yet to match where they were in the area of technological advancement. Should our enemies create another such advantage over us, it is likely the alien races already encountered this and created a means of countering it. Do not be so prideful as to not look to them for the answers.

The first point made had been in practice for centuries, so it was of no help to the current situation. They were currently putting the second point into action, so that left only the last one to be of any use.

"Penavel, prepare my ship for immediate departure. Destination, Silosan Three," he ordered via comlink.

"Yes, Majesty."

One of the few places in existence that contained remnants of the alien civilizations that had once dominated the galaxy, the third moon of Silosan was home to an imperial research base investigating those remnants. Discoveries made there led to the creation of the empire's plasma weapons, so it was the best place to start looking for a defense against these new railguns. If not, it was possible to find what they needed to build their own guns.

The only other location he knew where alien technology might still exist was Asilon IV, but that was a bigger gamble. The planet was held by the union in the past, and they never found anything, nor had the empire made any discoveries since acquiring it. A small contingent kept the planet safe from anyone else that might come looking, but nothing was being done there for the moment.

Still, if Silosan III didn't work out, he'd have to make a trip there to see if he could find anything for himself.

GCS Reno

3:03 P.M.

Originally intending to get some work done on New Hope, Leon ended up spending only a short time there before leaving once again. He wasn't one to sit still for very long, and action was required now more so than bureaucracy anyway. Besides, it wasn't like he couldn't get things done from the ship as well as from his office on the planet.

"Enter," he said in response to the door chime.

"You wanted to see me, sir," Major Breise stated after stepping up to the desk.

"I've been thinking about your team and its part in this war. The last operation you went on was to capture the Ordonian dreadnaught, and since then your main priority has been to locate any other Guardians, correct?" the president questioned, referring to members of the special forces branch of the former Vehlan Union.

"Yes, sir."

"How's that going?"

"I believe we have actionable intel on the locations of two teams. We also have leads on the whereabouts of three other teams, but need to go in the field to hunt them down. I requested to do so, but Major Mathison insists we stay on standby in the event we're needed on a higher priority mission," Breise explained.

"Good. I've put together a team to take over for you. They will start with the actionable intel, then they will track down the other leads and continue the search for any more."

"With all due respect, sir, I'd like my team to handle this. We're the only ones that know enough about Guardian operations to safely track them down. Not only that, but they're our brothers and sisters. I can't sit idly by while they're in need."

"I understand how you feel, but I have another task for you. However, I am reassigning Private Exodus to this new team. He's spent enough time with you to bring a valuable perspective to the hunt."

"Private Exodus is a member of my team now, sir."

"He isn't an Azul Guardian."

"Even so, I consider him a member of my team."

"Why?" Tyquese questioned. The major didn't respond right away, appearing unsure of what to say, and the president leaned back in his chair to allow him a moment to gather his thoughts.

"He was with us for quite some time on Swarnlia, long enough for him to become part of the group. I even started training him as a prospect for the guardians, and it didn't feel right to give up on him once we got out."

"It is that exact training we need on the other team. There may come a day when he joins the guardians, but until then he can't be a permanent part of your team," Leon insisted.

"Understood, sir. What about the rest of us?"

"I'm assigning you to be General Tyquese's personal security detail."

"I mean no disrespect, Mr. President, but isn't that overkill? Wouldn't we be better suited in the field?"

"You will be in the field. We cannot conduct this war out of hidden bunkers, far from the sight of our soldiers on the battlefield. We face enormous odds, and every soldier knows that. The general and I need to be out where we can be seen, and if I know my brother, that also means fighting alongside them. A normal security detail will not suffice for these conditions. I need the best watching out for him, as they will be in the thick of it," Leon assured him.

"Understood, sir. We'll keep him safe."

"I know you will. Dismissed."

GCS Victory
Friday, March 19th, 2709
7:12 A.M.

The tactical screen displayed every last detail of the Merchant's Interest, and Sam examined every pixel to determine if any preparations remained before starting the invasion. Their best hope of success lay in strong tactics and flawless execution and he wasn't about to let them lose because of a failure to pay attention on his part.

There was little doubt in his mind that the empire was going to use attrition as its main defense of the Interest. If they brought in more fleets to force them out it would weaken the defenses around other imperial holdings, but a full retreat would ascribe strength to the confederacy in direct contradiction of their propaganda.

No, they were going to hold out as long as possible, doing as much damage as they could in the meantime. In doing so, they would effectively destroy the Interest's economy, making it useless to the confederate war effort.

By knowing the Ordonian plan, Sam could counter it. Instead of launching a full-out invasion of every system, he was going to do things a little more conservatively.

He would start by securing the spaceways of each outlying system and stranding the Ordonian ground units within each one. This wouldn't be too difficult since they had already defeated the main fleet and the majority of the remaining ships had retreated to the home system of Merchanta.

Once that was done, he would ignore those ground targets for the time being and attack Merchanta itself. The space battle there would be a challenge, but victory was attainable. It was the ground battle he was concerned about.

Upon securing orbit, three-quarters of the fleet's infantry personnel would shuttle down to the planet and take over the enemy bases. When the rest of the planet was secured, they would lay siege to the capital with the purpose of liberating it for the merchants.

The problem was that the imperial garrison equaled the size of the confederate attack force, and they were protected by defensive fortifications while the attackers would be exposed. The only way they were going to win this battle was with cunning and determination.

Finally satisfied that everything was in place, the general walked onto the bridge and gave the order which erupted into a flurry of activity as the crew prepared for battle.

Silosan III
8:00 A.M.

The emperor stepped up to the transport ramp and looked down to find two of his personal guards confronting a man in a beige suit, the director of the Granthem Research Facility. They verified his id off his palco, then stepped aside to make room for the emperor and master knight.

"Don't bother with pleasantries, Director. Do you have anything to report?" Lentaise demanded before the other could say anything.

"We looked through all our research for anything related to railgun technology but didn't find any data related to the weapons described by Primary Canza."

"I'm not interested in what you've previously discovered, I want to know if you've found any leads in what's left to be studied," Lentaise replied impatiently. The director clasped his hands together in a visible effort to stop them from shaking and when he spoke it was with considerable effort.

"There is nothing left, Majesty. We have deciphered all the records and reverse engineered all of the equipment."

"You're telling me our current level of technology matches that of the aliens we fought over four hundred years ago?"

"Yes, Majesty. At least when it comes to the aliens that inhabited this planet."

"*Why* am I just now hearing about this? We have a war to fight, and we're sinking money and resources into pointless research!" Lentaise roared, causing the director to shrink away from him.

"That's not true. What I mean to say is, there are still things we can learn to upgrade our existing systems. I should have said there are no new technologies to be discovered."

Seething with anger, the emperor stood staring at the man while deciding his next move. He wasn't happy to learn the value of this facility had been exaggerated, but if new upgrades were to be found, he couldn't simply shut it down.

"Go inside and prepare a full presentation on your current research and expected progress," he finally ordered.

"As you wish, Majesty," the director acquiesced, then bowed and practically ran inside the adjacent building, nearly tripping over himself in the process.

"It is the duty of the Star Knights to oversee all top secret research on my behalf, Penavel. Why wasn't I informed of this?"

"I don't know, but I intend to find out," Penavel responded in an ominous tone.

"What about Asilon IV? Are there any surprises waiting for me there?"

"Nothing has been found to warrant stationing a Star Knight at that location."

"Send one now. Make sure I don't waste more of my time making a pointless trip."

"Yes, Majesty," Penavel replied.

He left the master knight on the landing pad then and walked down the carbocrete path to the facility, hardly noticing his surroundings as he considered his next move.

His first idea had fallen through, but he wasn't going to let that stop him.

He'd defeated the Vehlans. He would defeat the confederates.

It was only a matter of time.

Chapter Five
Deceptions

Camp Adamant
Saturday, March 20th, 2709
8:42 A.M.

"Get me a comlink to General Tyquese, *now*!" Captain Turley shouted without bothering to use his office's intercom.

Their greatest advantage was in imminent danger of being discovered by the Ordonians, which would likely spell their doom if they couldn't find a way to defend it. They had only managed to hold on to it this long by using a deception to keep the enemy's attention away, but it had always been a matter of time before the ruse was found out.

That time had come.

A sergeant reported the comlink was ready moments before the general's face appeared as a hologram above his desk.

"General, I just learned that a Star Knight is on his way to Asilon IV," Turley reported.

"How could you possibly know this?" Tyquese questioned, and Turley responded by giving him a look that said he should know better.

"I find it hard to believe you have an informant in the knights," the general pressed.

"No, but I do have many in the regular military, including the logistics department which the knight just ordered to provide him with a transport."

"I see. Well, we knew this would happen eventually. Take care of it."

"What are you talking about?"

"I'm too far away to do anything, so I'm trusting you to handle it."

"You know I operate by manipulating things behind the scenes. I'm not the one to lead a full-scale defense!"

"No, you're not. Even if you were, a full-scale defense is not an option here. The only way out of this is through clever deception, not force of arms. You are the most qualified officer under my command for that task."

"To be clear, you are giving me full authority to enact any plan I come up with?"

"Yes."

"Understood, General," Turley said, then cut the connection. He then ordered the orbiting gunship to prepare for immediate departure before going to work on a letter to the commander at Asilon.

An idea for deceiving the knight was already unraveling in his mind, but he would have to work out the details on the way. Whatever his plan ended up being, it had to look like the confederates were never there, which meant deconstructing the base and hiding the entrance to the alien facility. Those tasks had to be started right away, which he stressed in the letter.

At least it would take the knight a couple days to travel from Ordeos, while Asilon IV was only a short trip of a few hours from the asteroid Turley currently inhabited.

He sent the letter, then departed the command center for the shuttle that would take him to the gunship.

His mood improved as he walked, and a passing trooper gave him a curious glance due to the mischievous smile that was no doubt now on his face.

He did enjoy a good challenge, and the task of deceiving a Star Knight would not be lacking in that area.

GCS Reno
Monday, March 22nd, 2709
11:29 A.M.

The confederacy's youth and focus on the war meant there were few presidential duties, so Leon had decided to personally lead an invasion of the Magnin Kingdom.

The kingdom was one of the two nations recently conquered by the empire, and it was invaded by Emperor Lentaise himself. Its liberation would bruise the emperor's ego, possibly causing him to act rashly and make a mistake, but the Magnins were also a relatively strong nation who could be a significant asset to the confederacy.

An Ordonian by birth, Grives Magnin desired the throne for himself and led an assassination attempt against the emperor nearly two-hundred years ago. When he failed, he fled to a region of minor nations and lawless territories on the empire's border where he managed to establish a power base and unite all of them under his rule. His successors had opposed the Ordeon Empire ever since.

The only reason it had taken the Ordonians this long to conquer them was because it had always considered the Vehlan Union on its opposite border a much larger threat.

Magnin had brought quite a lot of imperial culture with him, as well as military tactics and discipline. It was Leon's hope that his successors would be able, and willing, to put all of that to use in helping the confederate war effort.

The decision to launch this attack also came from the fact Leon now felt the need to make the empire think the confederacy was stronger than was true. Presenting themselves on two fronts would serve this purpose, as well as keep the empire off-balance.

This resulted in stretching their forces to the limit and weakening their defenses in some areas, but the president had concluded it was an acceptable risk. Sam had concurred.

"Approaching target coordinates now, sir."

"Time to give the emperor a bloody nose. Commence attack," Leon responded, eliciting some quiet laughs.

The fleet dropped out of hyperspace into the Magnin's first border system only to discover none of the Ordonian patrols were where they should be.

"It looks like there's already a battle under way," Tactical commented, confused.

"What's happening?"

"I'm reading a couple dozen civilian grade security spacecraft engaging an imperial destroyer and its escorts. They're in orbit over the third planet."

"I should have known the Magnins wouldn't give up so easily," Leon admitted with a smile, then asked, "How are they doing?"

"It looks like they were holding their own, but the Imps have gained the upper hand. It's only a matter of time before they wipe out the rebels."

"Bring us in. All ships, target the destroyer and open fire once we're in range."

They accelerated towards the enemy, but the Ordonians disengaged from the battle and escaped into hyperspace before the confederates could fire a single shot.

As soon as they were gone, the Magnin ships gathered in an attack formation and faced off against the newcomers, but chose to open communications before firing.

"This is Colonel Inzorn of the Magnin Militia to invading vessels. Identify yourselves," the message came through. Leon ordered a channel opened but for it to be kept audio only.

“This is Leon Tyquese of the Galactic Confederacy. We are not your enemy,” Leon responded. He decided it was best not to reveal the fact he was the president at this point.

“What's your intention here?”

“We are here to liberate the kingdom from the empire. I wasn't expecting your people to already be in open revolt, but now that I see you are, I would like to offer our assistance.”

“We don't need any help. Leave our territory immediately or be fired upon.”

“There's no way you can defeat the occupation forces on your own, and you certainly can't fight them and us at the same time.”

“We will not be subject to any foreign power. We will die first.”

“I assure you we have no intention of ruling over you. You are more than welcome to join the confederacy as an independent nation, but if you don't want to do this, we are still willing to help you free your people. Once that is accomplished, we will leave in peace,” Leon reassured him.

There was a short pause during which Leon wondered if the fiercely independent Magnins were capable of working with anyone else, regardless of the other side's intentions.

“Send some troops to end the ground battle, and I'll relay your offer to the general,” Inzorn finally relented.

“Agreed,” Leon responded, then signaled for the channel to be cut.

He ordered his people to send a single battalion to the planet's surface, figuring it would be enough to defeat the imperial garrison once combined with the rebel forces.

An open revolt already in progress would make the liberation of this nation easier, bringing its resources into the war on the side of the confederacy sooner.

He just hoped the Magnins didn't turn out to be as bad as the Ordonians.

OES Lentaise Four
Tuesday, March 23rd, 2709
5:33 A.M.

"You're leading the ground attack!" Knight Ricine asked in response to Primary Canza's declaration.

The fleet had secured orbit around the first target in its invasion of the Vaton Conglomerate when Primary Canza made his announcement. The target was small, minimizing the risk, but commanders at his level never led ground troops into battle and she couldn't believe he was trusting her enough to leave her in command of the fleet.

"That's correct. Your orders are to stay here and coordinate our efforts."

"Why are you doing this?"

"My reasons are my own. Now carry out your orders," he responded, then exited the bridge.

The conversation clearly over, she went to the tactical station and checked on troop readiness. Their target was an asteroid outpost, which shouldn't cause any trouble, but she wanted to make sure they were ready for anything since no one knew the full capabilities of the Vatons.

It would be a few more minutes before the ground attack force was ready, so the knight took a seat in the captain's chair and began checking on what the primary had been doing recently under the guise of a systems' check. Her official investigation was suspended, but her status as a Star Knight allowed her to make surface inquiries as she felt necessary.

She didn't find anything out of the ordinary, but still couldn't shake the feeling he was up to something.

6:01 A.M.

The lander bucked from near misses as anti-air defenses did their best to shoot them down, but Primary Canza showed no concern as he left his seat to stand by the port exit.

His platoon followed his lead and formed into lines, two at each door and the rear ramp, and he watched them knowing anything he felt was hidden by his helmet's face shield.

To date, this legion had fought only one battle, and not every member had participated. For many of those with him, this would be their first time seeing real action. They may have been trained from childhood, but no amount of training truly prepared you for that first firefight.

When he felt the transport slow, Canza returned his gaze to the door in front of him, confident these men and women would do their job no matter their amount of prior experience.

The door opened and he jumped outside ahead of his platoon which disembarked via all three exits. The gravity was low and there was no atmosphere, but weighted boots allowed them to move normally and all standard armor types were equipped with independent air supplies.

Upon seeing no sign of the enemy, he instructed his soldiers to set up a perimeter around the rim of the crater which held the outpost. Three other transports had also landed, one for each compass point, and their personnel rushed to close the gaps seemingly unaffected by the low-gravity conditions.

As they finished, Canza looked down towards the outpost itself, his position on the crater rim offering him the perfect vantage point, but he saw no activity.

No shots were fired.

Nothing moved.

He hadn't expected the operation to be difficult, but this was still part of the Vaton border defense and should be displaying some sort of activity.

It was suspicious to be sure, but they still had a job to do, so the primary ordered the first line forward and took his place at its head. As they descended into the crater, a second line stepped up to take their place on the rim and maintain the perimeter.

He kept their pace slow and carefully watched for any surprises, determined not to be blindsided by whatever the Vatons were planning.

Then he spotted movement on a rooftop which revealed an automatic turret taking aim in their direction.

"Take cover!"

The legionnaires dropped to the ground, narrowly avoiding a volley of plasma bolts as several turrets opened up.

They stopped moving, but the turrets weren't merely motion-activated so they continued firing with extreme accuracy and screams of pain flooded their headsets.

"Second line! Fire!"

Several rockets shot down from the rim and struck the turrets, destroying each of them in soundless flashes of light.

"Casualties?"

"Twenty-seven, sir."

Every muscle in Canza's body tightened and he jumped to his feet, but he restrained himself from charging into the base.

"How many of those are dead?" he asked the command post.

"Nine, sir."

He looked around at the soldiers loading their wounded comrades onto stretchers and rushing them up out of the crater, unable to remove their armor and treat them until they could get them back into an atmosphere.

The new armor had seemed invulnerable against the enemy lasers in the last battle, but not this time against plasma weapons. It was supposed to be equally effective against both, so he'd have to investigate that later.

"Resume march," he ordered.

Once inside the outpost, the legionnaires carefully poked around outside the buildings until they determined there weren't any more traps waiting for them, then Canza moved up to his first target and motioned a private forward to breach the door.

When he opened the door the legionnaire started to walk through, but Canza heard the faint sound of a motor turning.

He reacted quickly and pushed the man away from the door just as an interior turret fired. The private fell to the ground as the shot grazed the primary's arm without penetrating his armor.

"Thank you, sir."

The primary chose not to respond and instead ordered someone else to throw in a grenade.

He spun into the room immediately after it detonated, a legionnaire at his side and both their weapons pointed high.

The turret tracked towards Canza, but damage caused by the explosion slowed it down enough to give him time to fire and finish it off before it could lock on.

"All personnel, automatic turret discovered in first building. Proceed with extreme caution."

His platoon continued into the building, which proved to be a storage warehouse. They encountered two more turrets, but these were easily eliminated now that they knew to look for them.

However, they did not find a single Vaton.

He received similar reports from the platoon leaders when they met in the center of the outpost once it was fully secured.

They encountered several automatic turrets, but not one person. All equipment was either missing or destroyed.

"The cowards ran, but left their defenses to kill as many of us as possible," one lieutenant observed.

"It is not cowardice to refuse to fight a battle you know you can't win, but there is no reason other than spite to leave machines behind to kill your enemy in your stead," Canza commented.

Asilon IV
Thursday, March 25th, 2709
10:22 A.M.

"Take us in closer," Star Knight Quince ordered in response to the pilot's report of a debris field above the planet.

He watched the sensor display on the transport's console as they drew closer, but at this distance the debris was too small and scattered for them to provide any significant clues as to what happened.

"Any sign of the cruiser?" he questioned.

"Negative."

Still not close enough for a detailed scan of the debris, Quince held up his palm, activated his palco, and checked recent reports regarding this post. The last supply run was nearly two weeks ago, and all was reported to be going according to routine.

"Data coming in now, sir," the pilot reported. Instead of looking back at the console, the knight interfaced his palco to the ship's systems and used it to study the sensor readings.

The debris field was the right size for a medium cruiser, and enough pieces were still intact to hint at a cruiser's shape as well. Residual radiation indicated a power core explosion, which brought the possibilities of what destroyed the ship down to a malfunction, self-destruct, or sabotage.

"Any readings from the surface?" he finally asked after filing away the readings for inclusion in his report and deactivating his palco.

"Nothing in the vicinity of the base, but we are seeing a massive crater several kilometers to its west."

"Life signs?"

"Sporadic."

"Land near the crater, close to the largest concentration of life signs," Quince ordered, then stepped out and headed to his quarters at the craft's midsection.

He changed out of his uniform and into his armor, choosing to forgo the helmet this time, then slung a rifle over his back.

The uniform was sufficient when his mission was merely to inspect a small outpost, but now the risk was greater as were the chances of a fight.

He felt the slight thump of the transport touching down as he finished, so he left his quarters and approached the side door where the co-pilot was already waiting.

"Anything new to report?"

"We spotted some of our troops while on approach and landed nearby. The immediate area appears secure for the moment."

"Any signs of enemy incursion?" he checked, and the woman responded in the negative.

When the door opened, Quince was the first to look outside where he saw a lieutenant with three enlisted men standing in the short brown grass facing them. He quickly glanced around, then disembarked and walked up to them when he was certain there was no immediate danger.

"I don't care if you're a Star Knight, I'm still happy to see you. I'm not sure our remaining supplies could have lasted another two weeks," the lieutenant greeted him.

"What happened here?"

"There were some who felt we were abandoned out here, so they started talking about defecting. When the rest of us remained loyal, they staged a mutiny."

"Why wasn't anything mentioned in your reports?"

"There wasn't any way for them to leave this planet, so I concluded it was nothing but talk and it wasn't necessary to report idle complaints. That's all it was until we discovered the facility and they decided they could use it to bribe pirates for passage off-planet."

"What facility?" Quince questioned, and the lieutenant responded by waving an arm towards the crater.

"Show me," he demanded, then the two of them made their way to its edge while the others stayed with the ship.

Once at the rim, the knight looked down and judged it to be nearly twenty meters deep and three times as wide. The dirt was blackened all the way around and several wisps of white smoke continued to lazily curl into the air, one of which was coming from a piece of nearby debris which he climbed down to investigate.

He pulled out a scanner from a pouch on his belt then used it to scan the item along with some other smaller pieces. The results indicated unknown alloys with qualities beyond what the Ordonians, or anyone else, were capable of producing.

"Tell me everything that happened," he ordered without looking up.

"I assigned regular patrols in the interest of keeping everyone busy, and a few days ago a team detected radiation in this area that could only come from an artificial source. When they investigated further, they discovered a cave with a wall inside. We brought in the necessary equipment the next day and cut through to discover technology far more advanced than anything we'd ever seen," the lieutenant described.

"Why wasn't this discovery reported immediately?"

"I tried, but mutineers aboard the cruiser intercepted my message. Then, those here on the surface attempted to subdue those of us still loyal, but we fought back. We managed to fight them back to the facility itself, and shortly afterwards it exploded. I'm still not sure if the mutineers purposely did it, or if one of our shots hit something and caused it."

"How was the cruiser destroyed?"

"The captain self-destructed before the mutineers could take control."

"What type of facility was this, and who built it?"

"I don't know, but it didn't look human to me, sir."

"You and the other survivors are to consider yourselves under an oath of silence on this matter. You will not discuss what you found or the resulting events with anyone, not even each other. Do you understand?"

"Yes, sir!"

There was nothing further, so Quince took one last look at the destruction then headed back to the transport.

The military didn't assign its best personnel to guard backwater planets, so the lieutenant's explanation was plausible. With nothing else to go on, he had to accept it as truth.

This planet was now worthless to the empire.

GCS Shadow
11:34 A.M.

The icon representing the knight's transport on the tactical screen disappeared in a flicker of white light to indicate hyperspace entry.

"They're gone," Captain Turley commented with no small amount of satisfaction. He had watched the whole thing from the safety of a Jammer Vessel's null field in orbit, and his plan had worked perfectly with the Star Knight coming and going without being any the wiser regarding their presence.

Plus, he had taken the "survivors" with him, granting the captain several more spies within the Ordonian ranks.

"Does that mean we can get back to work now?" the lead scientist studying the alien teleporter technology questioned from behind him.

"Yes, I'll have you and all your equipment shuttled back to the surface," Turley sighed.

"I still don't see why we had to evacuate. They didn't go anywhere near the device and we could have gotten a lot of work done while you conducted your little performance."

The captain swiveled his chair around to face the man and stared straight into his eyes as he delivered his response.

"There was always the chance my plan would fail and the knight would discover the facility. At that point I would have detonated the nuclear device that now sits beneath it, vaporizing it along with everything and everyone inside. Do you really feel that a few hours of work is worth your presence in that scenario?"

The scientist paled slightly, shook his head no, then hurriedly exited the bridge and the captain turned back towards his crew.

"Land the ship next to the facility and tell the transports to follow us down. Let's get this done as quickly as possible. We have our own work to get back to."

Chapter Six
Slaves No More

GCS Victory
Thursday, April 1st, 2709
7:23 A.M.

Over a thousand former Nosine slaves equipped with Vaton weaponry and decked out in Vaton armor stood before General Tyquese in the hangar bay, the bright white of the armor nearly blinding him with its active camouflage disabled. The four protectors assigned to him by Leon stood behind him on either side of a transport ramp in dark blue armor.

There were thousands more Nosines and Vehlans in the Victory's other hangars and even more in hangars of other ships in the fleet, all of them primed to charge onto Merchanta and drive off the occupiers.

For this attack, he had chosen not to use any troopers, electing to deploy them elsewhere. They were best utilized in raids and covert missions, not full-scale battles.

Mere months ago, over a quarter of this invasion force had been slaves, and the rest little more than refugees. Now here they all were, free and with homes, fighting together to preserve both of those things. There could be no finer testament to the human spirit.

The general suddenly realized he was starting to sound like his brother and suppressed a laugh before getting on with the business at hand.

"Normally, I am not one for making speeches, but this is one of those times where the occasion calls for it, so I am willing to make the effort.

"No one here comes from the world we are fighting to liberate today. I'm sure that many of you are wondering why you are putting your lives on the line to free a planet that is not yours while your own home remains under Ordonian power. When you think that, remind yourself that you *are* fighting for your home. This is but one step in what will be a long road towards ridding the galaxy of the Ordeon Empire's tyranny, ensuring peace for all mankind.

"Vehlans, you have already walked this road for a long time, longer than anyone else in this conflict. However, for much of that conflict, you were fighting for ideals you could not fully understand. Never before has Vehla been controlled by a foreign power, so its fight for freedom has never truly been personal. Now it *is* personal, and I know you will fight with your every breath to free your home and families.

"Nosines, you have been enslaved by the empire for nearly as long as it has existed. You know what it is like to be denied freedom while still yearning for it with your whole being. Today you take the second step towards gaining that freedom. Today you show the galaxy you are *not* slaves; you are *not* lesser than everyone else. Today you stand up as equals to fight side by side with those who believe as you do. I know you will tell the empire that you will be slaves no longer!

"Together, we will *all* tell the Ordonians we will allow them to go no further! The line has been drawn, and it is now time for justice to be done!"

He finished by yelling and raising his rifle into the air, and the troops did the same, rattling the walls with the power of their combined determination.

General's Transport
8:02 A.M.

The craft finally stopped shaking from the rapid descent, but then it started up again from the nearby explosions of anti-air shots. Most of the ground-based weapons were destroyed in a preceding wave of bombers, so they were able to continue on their way in relative safety.

He could have bombed their targets from orbit, but no targeting system was accurate enough to guarantee precise shots from that distance and he wanted to take the enemy bases mostly intact.

His own attack force was going after the main Ordonian position several kilometers north of the capital, and he could see it now from his position in the cockpit.

Columns of black smoke dotted with flickers of orange spiraled into the air to cast gloom on an otherwise bright and sunny day. The largest ones marked the locations of demolished hangars while the smaller ones indicated destroyed gun emplacements.

He could also see several crumpled vehicles and plenty of random debris, but he knew better than to think this fight was anywhere near over.

The majority of the base's infantry garrison would have survived the bombing by taking shelter in underground bunkers to await the arrival of confederate ground troops and they would be supplied by similarly protected armories.

He was glad they had at least been able to take out nearly half of the imperial air power. The other half wouldn't pose much of a problem, at least not for the infantry.

"Landing sequence," the co-pilot reported.

With less than a minute to touchdown, Sam left the cockpit and went to the back of the transport, his escorts shadowing his every step. As he passed them, each of the hundred Nosines present stood and formed up behind them.

There were two types of troop insertion transports, the quick-deploy and standard models. The quick-deploy, also referred to as a dropship, didn't land, but instead flew approximately ten meters over a drop zone and opened hatches under the feet of the soldiers in its hold, literally dropping them onto the battlefield. A small tractor beam above each soldier slowed his descent enough to prevent injury.

The standard model, often called a lander, did land on a battlefield and off-loaded its personnel by ramp. It was also capable of carrying equipment for quick-deploying command posts, and it was one of these that Sam was now on. There were also dropships in his unit, but they were deploying troops directly into the base while the landers were deploying on the perimeter.

Mere seconds from touchdown now, Sam couldn't help but have a flashback to childhood, his older brother Leon dragging him along to military preparation camps while he insisted he didn't want to have anything to do with the military. A few years later he was in the recruitment office, getting ready to join because he felt he had no other choice, but he did have a choice at that moment between the fleet or infantry. He chose the fleet, solely because Leon was already in the infantry.

Yet here he was, preparing to lead an infantry battle.

Not long after becoming a pirate, Sam learned the only way to be successful was to be good at everything, so he taught himself to be a strong infantry soldier and commander. He was more than capable of leading this attack, but there was still that moment when the irony of the situation struck him.

A klaxon sounded, the transport touched down, the ramp lowered, and Sam led the charge onto the still frozen ground.

Some weapons fire came out of the base towards them, but the Vehlan Fox Tanks were doing a good job of keeping the enemy pinned down. These were light tanks with four armored wheels which were equipped with rapid-fire weaponry and were primarily used for anti-infantry duties.

He took a quick look around to ensure the area was secure then directed the setup of a headquarters behind the four landers that had carried his battalion. Heavy Vehlan tanks filled in the gaps between the vessels to create a solid barrier between them and the enemy.

They had their beachhead. Now it was time for the hard part.

Dropship Five
8:23 A.M.

A buzzer sounded in the dropship to signal one minute to target and Private Eric Olian gripped his rifle tight in anticipation. His laser rifle and pistol had been replaced with Vaton plasma variants, and this was his first time carrying them into battle. They weighed more than his old gear, making them feel alien as he held them, but they would become familiar soon enough.

His armor was still the same except for the helmet, so at least he didn't have to learn how to move in it again. The helmet was a new model sporting a full faceshield which provided more protection against shrapnel and also allowed for an air filtration system.

The camouflage pattern was also different from before by his own choice, which was easily done thanks to the adaptive camouflage program. This program scanned the area around a soldier and updated the colors and patterns to match when it was active, but the rest of the time the appearance was static and used to indicate the nation to which a soldier belonged.

However, the confederacy had yet to come up with its own design and didn't seem to care if its soldiers personalized their armor. Most of the others still kept the faded green of Vehlan armor, but after learning of their home planet's refusal to join the confederacy, Eric had decided he wasn't fighting for them any longer. He was fighting out of principle, not out of obligation.

The primary color of his armor was the grey of a misty day while the secondary and tertiary colors were white and black, each color blending seamlessly into its neighbors.

He was angry at Vehla, but despite how it had betrayed him and the others it was still his home, so he'd placed a blue circle on the back of each hand to commemorate it.

Across the drop bay from him stood his best friend, Private Jeremy Fields, who wore a matching camo design. When the ten second chimes sounded, Jeremy gave him a mock salute and he returned it before gripping his rifle again.

The hatch below him swung open to send him plummeting into open air and he quickly looked down to see where he was about to land.

As the ground rushed up to meet him, the dropship's tractor beam engaged to slow his descent. When it released him a meter above the surface he formed into a ball and rolled away out from under the craft.

Once back on his feet, he made sure Jeremy was with him before looking around for their lieutenant. When they saw her she was signaling the platoon to follow her to a nearby building and they jogged across the carbocrete to join her.

Gunshots and explosions echoed around the base, but they saw no imperials in their immediate vicinity. Smoke swirled around them, occasionally blocking their vision but not affecting their breathing thanks to the new helmets which allowed them to maintain a swift pace.

They reached the side of the building and stopped a moment to survey the situation and learned they had come up beside the control tower for the base's spaceport. The port itself was in ruins thanks to the bombing runs, but the tower still looked to be in pretty good shape. They could hear gunfire coming from the other side facing the tarmac, but nobody was shooting at them yet.

"The Ordonians have set up firing positions near the top of the tower, and it looks like they've got several of our people pinned down. Those soldiers were part of the attack on the command center, and without them it's less likely we'll be able to get it," the lieutenant announced, most likely learning this via a private comlink with the general's command post.

"Let's get 'em!" Fields enthused.

"Wait," Olian objected when he saw the lieutenant about to order them in.

"What is it?"

"Why aren't they covering this side of the tower?"

"Why would they be? There's nothing over here," another soldier commented.

"True, but these are Ordonians we're talking about here. It's not like them to leave themselves wide open like this," Olian responded.

"He's right. They probably have an ambush waiting for us inside. Anyone got a drone?" the lieutenant finally agreed.

"I do," Olian answered, pulling a small reconnaissance drone out of a pouch on his belt and offering it up. She took it, activated it, then sent it to fly in through the nearest door.

A video feed appeared on the inside of their faceplates as the drone maneuvered through the door but it dissolved into static before showing them anything on the other side, then a small spherical object came sailing through to land on the ground in front of them.

"Grenade!" the lieutenant shouted.

The soldiers covered their heads, but she scooped it up and threw it as far as she could before throwing herself to the ground.

A wave of heat from the resulting explosion washed over them, but their armor easily deflected it to prevent injury.

As soon as the blast dissipated, Fields took out a grenade of his own and tossed it inside, then turned away just as a fiery blast came roaring out.

"Breaching!" the soldier nearest the door shouted as he ran into the smoke.

Gunfire erupted the moment he passed inside and some of the white plasma bolts streaked through the door, but the others followed him without hesitation.

The fifth one to go through, Olian ducked to the left, saw something move on the other side of the room, so he took a shot at it without slowing down.

Not waiting to see if he hit his mark, the private quickly looked around for some cover and spotted another Vehlan ducking behind a desk. He started to follow, but was just drawing near when the desk and soldier disappeared in a fireball.

The explosion threw him onto his back, and his head hit the floor – hard. His armor prevented him from getting hurt, but the force of the impact still stunned him.

He knew he couldn't just lie there and let down his friends, so he rolled onto his right side which allowed him to see a barricade on the other side of the room. It was constructed from prefabricated panels which included firing slots, all of which were manned by zealous Imps flooding the room with plasma bolts.

Hoping they wouldn't notice him, the private aimed his rifle at one of the slots and fired. His aim proved true, and he saw the soldier on the other side fall back.

Another Vehlan spotted the opportunity and threw a plasma incendiary grenade through the same slot, the fire of which was hot enough to burn through most armor types.

The grenade went off and screams of intense pain replaced the gunfire until several Vehlans ran up to the barricade and stuck their weapons through the slots and put those on the other side out of their misery. They stayed there and kept watch while cutting teams moved up to make a way through.

“Are you just going to lie there for the rest of the battle?” a voice cut through the fog in Olian's head and he rolled onto his back again to see Fields standing over him.

“I was considering it,” Olian quipped.

He accepted his friend's hand up, then looked over at the desk where he had intended to take cover but only saw a smoking hole in its place.

“What happened?” he asked.

“Looks like the Imps planted a proximity mine behind that desk. It went off when someone tried to take cover there.”

“I saw him. I was about to take cover with him. Did he make it?”

“No,” Fields responded soberly, and Eric followed his gaze to a blackened, unmoving body plastered against the wall.

Fresh gunshots drew their attention back to the barricade, cutting short any time for mourning. The cutting teams hadn't made it through yet, so someone covering them must have spotted enemies trying to reinforce the position.

The two friends took their positions near the barricade and waited for the cutting teams to finish so they could get to the stairs on the other side. They could already access the elevators but they all knew they were most likely sabotaged.

Once they finished cutting, a member of each team knocked out the cut sections with a shoulder thrust or kick while others moved the equipment out of the way.

Several soldiers stormed through, jumped over enemy corpses then swept the room with their rifles on alert for any that were still living and dangerous.

The first ones through secured the area and those that followed cleared a path through the bodies and debris to make sure everyone could get through as quickly as possible.

Once the ground floor was deemed secure, two soldiers found the stairway entrance, blew it open with a breaching charge and stormed through, but they were cut down by weapon's fire from above.

Without hesitation, Fields launched himself through the door, landed on his stomach on the other side, and immediately started firing upwards.

Not about to let his friend get all the glory, Olian ran through the door and headed straight for the stairs, firing as he went with the others following him as they were able.

Some shots came their way, but Fields was able to keep the enemy pinned back, allowing the attackers to make their way up the stairs and to the next landing. A few of them went through the door to secure that level while the rest continued up.

At this point they were able to see several enemy soldiers running up the stairs ahead of them, firing behind them as they went. The Vehlans kept giving chase, with a few of them breaking off at each level to secure it.

The Ordonians exited the stairwell at the top floor with Olian right on their heels, but he didn't follow and instead secured the landing with the few who had made it this far with him.

They'd won this fight. No use getting killed now at the end of it.

Hilson
1:17 P.M.

The company of over one-hundred Nosines slowly entered a large traffic rotary and spread out in search of enemies, most of them heading to the center island to look behind the hedges. When he came in with the center of the group, Colonel Hikhan Janovich decided to take advantage of the break in fighting and ordered them to secure the area.

After he was made general, Sam Tyquese had officially commissioned the Nosine rebels as soldiers alongside the Vehlans, given Hikhan the rank of colonel, and tasked him with leading all the Nosine divisions.

All the other units involved in this battle were under the command of Vehlan officers, but here he was all on his own leading troops into the first real engagement for any of them.

He was assigned to secure a city the empire was using as a headquarters for this sector of the planet. The garrison here was relatively small, but it still needed to be dealt with before they could go after the capital.

So far they were making good progress, pushing the defenders back with minimal effort, but Hikhan knew it should never be this easy fighting Ordonians, even if he did happen to have more experienced soldiers in his command.

"Colonel!" a soldier shouted from a side street and Hikhan rushed over with several others.

"What is it?" he asked upon arriving, and the soldier responded by merely pointing down the street.

When he looked where the man was pointing, the colonel saw three enemy Atlas heavy tanks barricading the road before the next intersection along with two Fearmonger mechs which stood in between them. He could also see at least a dozen soldiers behind the vehicles.

"We've been surrounded!" another soldier reported over comms.

"Steady. Take up defensive positions and wait for my orders," Hikhan reassured his troops.

An Ordonian captain escorted by two soldiers emerged from between the tanks with the soldier on the right holding a pole with a white cloth tied to its top. They started making their way towards the Nosines, but Hikhan made no effort to meet them halfway, instead directing those around him in preparing a defense while he waited for the officer to come to him.

"You are surrounded by superior firepower. Surrender now and I promise you will be treated properly," the officer, a captain, said the moment he was in hearing range of the Nosines. He also stopped there, as if he didn't want to come any closer.

“This is not the first time we have faced your superior firepower, Ordonian. We aren't afraid of you anymore, and we aren't taking any more orders from you,” Hikhan challenged.

“You and your people are not soldiers. Our people have lived in peace with one another for centuries. The confederacy has lied to you for its own ends. Give up this senseless struggle and go back to living in peace.”

“Peace comes at too high a cost for my people. We were slaves to you, nothing but tools to be used up and thrown away. From now on, we choose our own future!”

“All your needs were met before and will be again. How is that a worse fate than death?”

“I find it strange that you chose to talk instead of charging in here and killing us all. Is it possible you aren't nearly as strong as you claim and you're too scared to fight us?” Hikhan taunted, evoking chuckles from among his soldiers.

“Have it your way,” the captain responded, then turned on one heel and started marching back towards his position, but Hikhan had no intention of letting him make it that far.

“Charge!” he shouted, then ran down the street with his escorts right behind him. A few of them who hadn’t spent much time off their homeworld tripped and fell from their own momentum, but the more experienced of them quickly closed the distance.

The captain and his two escorts turned to confront them, throwing the flag on the ground and raising their weapons, but it was already too late.

Hikhan grabbed the captain and threw him to the ground, two of his men subdued the escorts, and several more kept running towards the tanks and mechs, none of which had opened fire.

“You're coming with us,” Hikhan stated, then grabbed the captain by the collar and pulled him down the street.

Realizing they weren't going to get a clear shot, the tanks went into reverse while the mechs stepped forward to slow down the rapidly advancing soldiers.

The mechs fired suppression rockets into the air which rained burning cinders down on the Nosines, but they felt nothing through their armor and sustained their pace.

Their first shots ineffective, the mechs switched to the low-powered pulse guns they had in place of hands, but those also had very little effect. They were equipped with more lethal weaponry, but weren't using it for fear of hitting their own people.

The Nosines reached the mechs and swarmed all over them, forcing them to the ground and prying open their cockpits to pull out the pilots, netting them two more prisoners.

The tank drivers, apparently deciding it was an acceptable risk, opened fire with their rapid-fire plasma guns which sent the Nosines scrambling for cover behind planters, benches, or whatever else they could find.

The colonel, still dragging his prisoner, hid behind a tree and looked back the way they had come where he spotted a pair of his soldiers with rocket launchers, so he waved them forward and ordered them to open fire.

They crouched where they were and fired, scoring one direct hit but the second just glanced off the tank's shield and exploded in the air.

Neither of them took any damage thanks to their heavy armor and shields, and they both disappeared around a corner before the Nosines could fire again.

Letting those three go for now, Hikhan handed the Ordonian captain off to another soldier and activated the tactical interface on his palco to check on the situation of the other units around the rotary.

None of them had prisoners they could use as shields, so they weren't doing nearly as well. In fact, it looked as though their positions were about to be overrun.

The colonel ordered them to fall back and regroup at his position, assigned some soldiers to watch his back, then returned with the rest to cover the retreat.

They took up position at the end of the street but didn't have enough time to set up a defense before the first retreating group reentered the rotary with white plasma bolts chasing them.

They looked around frantically until they saw Hikhan and took off for him at full speed.

A dozen Ordonians showed up seconds later and opened fire, shooting many before they could react.

"Return fire!"

Those with Hikhan opened up with everything they had, striking down some and forcing the rest into cover.

The fleeing Nosines ran past the colonel then turned and added their firepower to the defense.

Two more groups of Nosines showed up on the other side of the rotary, and also ran for the colonel, but this time the tanks that were chasing the first group were now in position to wipe them out.

"Colonel Janovich to command! I need air support at my location!"

"Specify your target."

He cursed under his breath, then pointed his rifle at the tanks and marked them with its targeting system.

"Target acquired. Twenty seconds out."

The tanks' main weapons were too slow to track footsoldiers, so the Ordonians pointed them towards the rotary's center and waited for the runners to come to them.

"We don't have twenty seconds!" a soldier cried out. Thinking fast, Hikhan could come up with only one solution.

"Drop now!" he shouted and the fleeing Nosines threw themselves to the ground where they covered their heads and stayed as low as possible.

Seeing this, but not understanding what was happening, two of the tanks turned their weapons towards Hikhan's position while the third reoriented itself to take out the now prone Nosines.

They never got the chance to fire.

Three missiles streaked out of the sky, striking the tanks and destroying them in a fantastic explosion which also gutted the surrounding buildings and sent enemy infantry running.

Three Vehlan Blackswords shot by overhead, eliciting cheers from the Nosines, all except for Hikhan who urged those still in the rotary to get moving.

"Where's the fourth group?" he asked the last man as he approached.

"They're gone."

With no one else coming, and no time to waste, the colonel rushed his soldiers towards an underground parking garage he'd spotted earlier.

Once there, they would link up with their own armor before returning to finish the fight.

Confederate Command Post
7:19 P.M.

"That was a risky move," General Tyquese told Hikhan via the monitor after he finished his report.

"What?"

"Your attacking the Ordonians while they were still under a flag of truce."

"I don't understand."

"They negotiated in good faith and trusted you to do the same according to the conventions of war."

"Since when do rules matter to a pirate?"

“The first thing a pirate learns is how to survive which means occasionally following the rules. If we do stuff like that too often, we run the risk of our troops getting killed while attempting to surrender.”

The colonel grew thoughtful, then nodded to show he understood.

“I'll contact you with new orders soon. Tyquese, out,” he concluded, then returned to viewing written reports on another monitor.

The setting sun cast an eerie glow throughout the command post, serving as a fitting backdrop to the end of the day's events. The fighting was long and intense, but the confederates had finally managed to secure most of the planet.

He had hoped to start the attack on the capital the next day, but as he looked at the casualty lists he knew that wasn't going to happen. They'd lost nearly a tenth of their ground forces today, and the rest were suffering from injuries and/or exhaustion. He'd made the mistake of overestimating the readiness of the Nosines for a fight such as this, and it had cost them.

The decision to wait brought with it the necessity to root out any remaining enemies on the rest of the planet or they ran the risk of them reorganizing and launching a counter-attack, but doing that would further delay the assault on the capital.

For the first time, he realized just how long of a war this would be.

Chapter Seven
Unraveling Threads

OES Lentaise Four
Tuesday, April 13th, 2709
10:41 A.M.

The Vaton border was fully secure, seized with relatively little effort and all appeared clear for the invasion to continue, but Canza had decided to wait long enough to determine a new strategy. He knew the conglomerate was better equipped to fight them than it had shown thus far and had come to suspect they were a far more guileful enemy than he had ever faced before.

"Primary Canza, there is a priority call for you from Vehla," the bridge reported via his office intercom.

"I'll take it here," he responded, then moved his work to the side to make room for the video feed.

"Governor Canza, I am contacting you for confirmation on an order from Emperor Lentaise. He has ordered us to open fire on the Vehlans, sir," the system's legion commander reported as soon as the connection was made.

"What target?"

"The general population."

"Did he give a reason?"

"Negative."

"Confirmation denied. Stand down," Canza told him.

"Are we to disobey a direct order from the emperor, sir?"

"Your orders come through me, Legion Commander, and I have received no such directive."

"Understood, sir."

Why would the emperor issue an order to randomly open fire on innocent civilians? The only thing that came to mind was a report earlier that morning of a rebellion in the Magnin Kingdom successfully defeating the occupying Ordonian forces with confederate help, but what did that have to do with Vehla?

It was the emperor who led the Magnin invasion, so he must be taking its liberation as a personal insult and clearly blamed the Vehlans.

Whatever the reason, he couldn't allow the slaughter of innocents in his jurisdiction, so he started a priority call to the palace on Ordeos and stood up while he waited for it to connect.

This call went through as a hologram which appeared above the primary's desk, and the first thing he saw was Master Knight Penavel whispering something in the emperor's ear who was seated in his office chair. A second later he backed off and Lentaise addressed the primary.

"Is it true you have countermanded my order regarding Vehla?" he questioned in a tightly controlled tone.

"Negative. I merely delayed the implementation of that order until I could speak with you," Canza responded.

"Then speak."

"My emperor, the Vehlans are not to blame for anything that has happened. They have accepted our rule, and are even starting to embrace it with many enlisting to serve in our military in response to your promotional campaign."

"The confederacy is led by Vehlans and they comprise a large part of their military."

"They are rogues, considered as such by their own people."

"There has to be a response to this outrage!" Lentaise shouted, leaping to his feat in his fury.

"I agree, Majesty. However, I have an alternative to attacking the people of Vehla," Canza told him.

"Explain."

"There are reports that Ascion is on the verge of joining the confederacy. It is a small nation, but they carry considerable influence with their neighbors and will likely use that influence to bring them into the war against us as well. We can prevent this by firestorming their homeworld, and this will also show all the nations the depth of our resolve."

Firestorming was an Ordonian tactic where they bombed a planet from orbit with supercharged plasma shots. The extra plasma didn't explode on impact but splashed like napalm which burned too hot to be easily extinguished. A precision bombing pattern created fires that would burn until a planet's entire surface was scorched bare.

Some had suggested they do this to Vehla after they achieved orbital control, but the emperor had decided he was more interested in their submission than their destruction.

Now that he had heard the plan, Lentaise slowly sat down again to consider it as Canza waited patiently.

"Very well. I rescind my order regarding Vehla. See to it that the firestorm is carried out," he finally agreed, then cut the connection once Canza confirmed the order.

The primary sat down and used the tactical interface on his desktop to assemble a small fleet using ships from his own invasion force then tasked it with attacking Ascion which sat on the conglomerate's other side.

When that was done, he sent a message to Secondary Zenzal containing orders to come to him immediately. He would need the secondary's support if his fears proved true.

No war was without its atrocities, some of them strategic actions taken in an effort to secure victory while others resulted from fear, anger, and hate. Emotions ran hot in any conflict, but it was the emperor's responsibility to set those emotions aside and do what was best for the empire. It was inconceivable for him to order a massacre simply because his pride was wounded, but that was exactly what he had just done.

If the legion commander had followed the order without contacting Canza they would have lost the loyalty of the Vehlan people along with everything they had accomplished.

Canza's first duty was to the empire and its people, then to whoever happened to be ruling it at the moment. He now found himself questioning if the two were still mutually compatible.

OES Lentaise Four
Friday, April 16th, 2709
2:22 P.M.

The secondary skirted around the bridge's main section and approached the office door on its right where he pushed the buzzer to make his presence known. It opened and he walked through and straight up to the desk where he stood at attention without saying anything, simply waiting for Canza to acknowledge him.

As he waited, he wondered once again why he had been summoned here. Normally the primary would just send him a message containing new orders and left him alone the rest of the time. With so much going on with the war, it was highly irregular for him to want to meet in person.

A few minutes after Zenzal entered the room, Canza found a stopping point in his work, then rose from his chair and walked to the front of his desk to stand facing his guest. He pulled a device from a front pant pocket, activated it, then placed it on the desk where the secondary could clearly see it.

It was a jamming device, meant to counter any spy devices that might have been placed in a room.

"Relax. We are not talking as soldiers right now, but as concerned citizens of the empire," Canza finally said.

He wasn't sure how he should react at first, but then he relaxed and turned to face his superior.

"What's going on, sir?"

"Several times in your career you chose to disobey direct orders because you felt they were detrimental to the mission. Why?"

"I believe it is every citizen's responsibility to think for himself and question any inappropriate actions on the part of our leaders."

"Do you still believe this?"

"Yes, I do. It is the only way to fight corruption," Zenzal answered passionately. It was possible the primary was about to discipline him for these actions and beliefs, but he wasn't about to back down.

"That's exactly what I need from you right now. Did you hear about the recent order Emperor Johan gave concerning Vehla?"

"No, sir."

"He ordered our troops to open fire on the general population because the confederacy helped liberate the Magnin Kingdom."

The news left Zenzal speechless, and his mind spun as he struggled to find some way to justify such an act, anything to escape the possibility he was serving an insane monarch.

Despite the fact they were at war with them only two years ago, the people of Vehla were now citizens of the Ordeon Empire. The idea of an emperor massacring imperial citizens was unthinkable, even in the event of an open revolt .

"I convinced him not to proceed, but the fact he would give such an order has me concerned. If Emperor Johan Lentaise becomes a threat to the empire, then we must be ready to act," Canza continued and Zenzal braced himself against the desk to keep from falling over.

"You're talking about overthrowing the emperor!"

"We are at a vital point in our quest to unite the human race. When we defeat the confederacy there will be no one left to challenge us."

"That's what we thought about the union," Zenzal remarked, but Canza ignored him.

"A single mistake could spell our defeat, and humanity will be thrown into a chaos that it might never recover from. I'm not going to let that happen."

"It's never been done."

"The Star Knights may be relatively few in number, but their reputation has always proven a barrier to gathering support. Now we have the legionnaires, any one of which is a match for a knight in single combat, a fact we can use to alleviate fear of reprisals. All we have to do is get the right political allies and not get caught."

"Don't you have a Star Knight as your second-in-command over the legionnaires?"

"Yes, and that is one reason why I need your help. Observing her is providing me with information about the knights, but she'll notice if I start cultivating political allies."

"So you are wanting me to contact potential supporters on your behalf?"

"Will you do this?"

"You're not ordering me to help you?"

"That is an order I cannot give," Canza professed.

The secondary turned his head to look at the framed flag hanging behind the primary's desk, specifically at the seal of the emperors in the center of the solid red background.

If it wasn't an order, he would be without excuse before the law should he choose to help. He would be subject to the same penalties, which would be death for him and most likely exile for his family.

However, Canza did have a point. The emperor's order to shoot imperial citizens was inexcusable, and it showed that his judgment may be flawed. If he made a foolish decision and they didn't act, it could cost the empire this war, a fate worse than death.

"I'm with you," he finally said. His gaze lingered on the flag a little longer, then he looked back at Canza to see him watching him with a sad smile.

"Return to your duties, but don't leave the ship. We'll discuss details later, but I won't be using this again, so choose your words carefully," Canza said as he picked up the jammer. Zenzal nodded to show his understanding then left the office.

Upon nearing the bridge exit, he spotted Knight Ricine standing there as if she had been waiting for him, her formal grey uniform standing out next to the crew's dark red jumpsuits.

"I wasn't expecting to see you during this mission, Secondary Zenzal," she commented.

"You should work on that lack of foresight," Zenzal responded flippantly as he continued towards the exit, but she blocked his way.

"What did Canza want with you that couldn't be accomplished with a comlink?"

"He's testing my loyalty to the empire and himself. He was sure about Farra but I have yet to earn that level of trust. A video screen or hologram doesn't reveal everything," he responded.

It was true – after a fashion.

"Wise of him, considering your background. I am left to wonder why he promoted you in the first place, however."

"I've proven my worth, in more ways than one."

"Yet here he is testing your loyalty. Why now?"

"It wasn't necessary while Farra was still around. Since his death, the primary has been very busy, and hasn't been able to find time to do this until now," Zenzal explained.

She seemed to think that over, then finally stepped out of his way. He expressed his annoyance with one last look, then proceeded to exit the bridge.

Things are going to get interesting quick if she already suspects us.

Chapter Eight
Burning

Ascion
Saturday, April 17th, 2709
12:03 P.M.

"So, what are your thoughts on us joining the Galactic Confederacy?" Seth questioned.

"I say we should stay out of it," Matt replied. The two of them were on their lunch break, walking to a nearby restaurant as they did every day.

"Really? Why?"

"It has nothing to do with us. The fight was between the Ordonians and Vehlans. When that finally ended, there was a chance for peace, but now this confederacy has appeared to stir things up again. Not only that, but they're trying to drag everyone else into it too."

"What about those other nations the empire attacked, like the Merchant's Interest. Seems to me they're gunning for everybody, so everybody needs to make a stand."

"Nobody can conquer the entire galaxy. If they tried, they would overextend themselves and fall apart from the inside out. Now if the Ordonians really are trying to do this, I say we just ride it out until that happens."

"Sounds awfully selfish to me."

The droning of emergency sirens interrupted their conversation, stopping Seth as he was opening the restaurant door. His hand still on the handle, he gave his friend a quizzical look, but Matt looked to be just as confused as he was. None of the others around them appeared to have any clue as to what was going on either.

The sky was overcast but the clouds were thin, and it wasn't time for a scheduled test of the sirens, so what could possibly be going on?

As everyone stood there gawking, the sirens droned on, their warning ignored.

Suddenly the door and all the windows exploded, sending everyone diving to the ground for cover where they were showered with shards of glass.

"Are you okay?" Seth yelled.

Matt lifted his head from the ground and gave a nod before the both of them carefully got back on their feet. Others around them did the same, and they could see there were no serious injuries.

Children inside cried while their parents attempted to hush them despite their own shaky voices, but it appeared no one was hurt in there either.

"What happened?" Matt questioned, but before anyone could respond, the ground shook, forcing them to brace themselves against whatever was near.

"Earthquake?"

"No! Look!" a young man shouted while pointing to the sky, a woman's arms wrapped around him.

Following the finger, Seth felt his breath catch in his throat.

"No...," someone whispered next to him.

The clouds were dissolving into wisps of vapor as dozens of white lights passed through them on their way to the city.

"Looks like the empire made up our minds for us," Seth commented.

"But we haven't chosen a side yet!" Matt shouted over the roar of a nearby explosion.

"Come on!" Seth urged as he pulled his friend towards him.

He looked to the west where he spotted a large column of smoke, so he took off running the other way with Matt following close behind.

As they ran, the explosions came faster and closer.

"Help! Help me!"

The scream pierced through all other noise, freezing Seth in his tracks. He looked around frantically for the source.

"What are you doing?" Matt called back, having stopped a couple meters in front of him.

The cry had come from an older woman who was trapped under a metal pole, so Seth ran over to help. He tried with all his might to lift the pole, grunting with the exertion, but it was too heavy.

"We don't have time for this! We need to get out of here!"

"Stop complaining and help me!"

Matt hesitated, looked around them as if expecting bad guys to appear at any moment, but then he finally knelt beside his friend and grabbed the pole. With their combined strength, the pole began to rise.

On the other side, an old man ran up and pulled the woman out, who then scrambled to her feet and ran off.

"*Now* can we get out of here?" Matt yelled, and Seth replied by running off.

Debris rained down from above, narrowly missing the two and covering them with dust, but they kept pushing forward.

A column of smoke rose into the sky ahead of them, so Seth switched directions, only to find more smoke that way.

He skidded to a stop, then turned in place to see nothing but smoke in all directions. Closer to him, people were running in all directions, but none of them seemed to know where to go.

The two of them ducked into an alleyway to catch their breath. As he leaned against a wall, Seth realized he couldn't hear any vehicle sirens. All he could hear was the constant drone of the city sirens broken up by explosions. Why weren't any emergency responders out?

"There's nowhere to run," he finally stated between gasps.

“So what are we going to do?” Matt gasped, the desperation plain in his voice.

A nearby building erupted into a huge fireball, knocking the friends to the ground once more.

They covered their heads and stayed down as debris rained down around them, the alley sheltering them from the worst of it.

When it cleared, Seth got back to his feet only to find fire and smoke in all directions.

“There's nothing we *can* do.”

“No! I don't want to die!” Matt declared.

He ran further into the alley where he found a door, which he then kicked open before running inside. Seth followed and the two of them made their way into the basement where they found themselves alone and in the dark with the temperature quickly rising.

GCS Reno

1:05 P.M.

Still in orbit above the Magnin homeworld, Leon hoped to persuade the kingdom to join the confederacy, or at the very least lend support to the fight. He was currently in his quarters reviewing transcripts of his conversations with their leadership, looking for anything that might help in further negotiations.

So far, he hadn't found much success. He'd managed to convince them to let his forces patrol the borders, but that was as far as it went.

The Magnins hated the Ordonians with every fiber of their being, but they were also extremely distrustful of everyone else. As such, they were more than willing to continue attacking the empire, but they weren't going to coordinate their efforts with anyone.

He finally resigned himself to the fact that this was the way it was going to be and decided to try for a different goal. If the Magnins weren't willing to coordinate military efforts, they might at least be willing to share what they knew of Ordonian tactics.

"Mr. President, we're receiving a distress call from the planet Ascion!"

"On my way," Leon responded as he rushed out, then demanded a report upon stepping onto the bridge.

"An imperial fleet destroyed all their defenses and is now bombarding the planet."

"Show me," Leon ordered as he took the captain's chair.

When the tactical view came up, courtesy of a link with Ascion's own satellites, he saw a small imperial fleet in orbit above the planet. The planetary defenses were wiped out, and the nearest reinforcements, confederate or otherwise, were hours away.

This was usually when the Ordonians sent in a ground invasion force, but this time they were just sitting in orbit, bombing the planet. That was when Leon realized what they were doing.

"They're being firestormed."

Silence fell over the bridge.

Everyone stopped what they were doing and stared at the main display.

A firestorm was a death sentence for a planet. It was a message that resistance would not be tolerated.

"What are we going to do?"

"Order all nearby troopers to the planet. Have them evacuate as much of the population as they can. They are not to engage the enemy," Leon ordered.

"Aren't we going to stop them?"

"They're hoping we'll try, but we aren't going to fall for their trap. We will save as many as we can, but not by sacrificing our means of fighting this war. Deactivate main screen," Leon responded before leaving the bridge.

It pained him to leave the people on that planet to the not so tender mercies of the empire, but there was nothing he could do without sacrificing the larger war effort.

When the Ordonians seized orbital control of Vehla, the union threw everything it had at them in one attack after another, but each one failed. Once so many of their resources were gone, they no longer had any hope of victory.

He was not going to make the same mistake twice.

Neither was he going to do nothing at all.

He returned to his quarters where he sent orders to the Vaton Conglomerate's special forces, tasking them with sabotaging and eventually eliminating the empire's mercenaries. Their raids on confederate supply lines were getting worse, and it was time they dealt with them.

He also sent orders to a trooper squadron placing it at the disposal of the Vaton team, then he ordered the rest into imperial space to conduct raids there.

He'd much rather have a team of Azul Guardians for this task, but the only team they had was guarding Sam. The people he had searching for any others had yet to come up with anything.

With that done, he began assembling a fleet for the express purpose of attacking Ordonian space. He would show them their brutal tactics would not be tolerated, and that the confederacy's resolve was absolute. Sam would lead the invasion once he was finished in the Merchant's Interest.

Imperial space had gone untouched long enough. It was now time to bring this war home to them.

Merchanta
1:39 P.M.

"We need to stop this!" Sam shouted at his brother, not caring if the others in his command post heard him.

"I've sent all available troopers to run the blockade and evacuate as many people as possible."

"That's not good enough!"

"Any ships we send in an attempt to drive out the enemy will be destroyed and we can't afford to lose them," Leon insisted, causing Sam to slap his hands on the table and lean closer to the monitor.

"You're thinking just like the union used to. We can't win by sacrificing people to save our ships."

"This is different from what happened at Palcion."

"It was our job to defend people then, but our leaders chose not to and our sister died as a result along with hundreds of thousands of others. The only difference I see is that there are a lot more who are going to die this time."

"We could have defended Palcion, but chose not to. By the time we assemble enough ships to overcome the Ordonian fleet, Ascion will already be a ball of ash," Leon explained.

As general, Sam knew this to be true, but he couldn't help thinking about all those people burning alive because of a fight that wasn't even theirs. Then he pictured Kate as one of them and clamped his eyes shut in an attempt to block the image.

"So we are supposed to just keep fighting this war as if those people don't matter?" he choked out.

"No. We fight even harder because they do matter."

Sam shoved himself away from the table and opened his eyes to look at the Merchant capital in the distance. He couldn't see them, but he thought about the Ordonian occupiers in their entrenched positions around the city and clenched his fists in anticipation of his attack.

"Yes. We will."

Chapter Nine
You're Not Wanted Here

Merchanta
Sunday, April 18th, 2709
5:47 A.M.

"Is everything in place?" General Tyquese asked without looking away from the tactical map.

"Yes, sir," Colonel Andrie confirmed.

Nodding slightly, the general returned to his thoughts.

No enemies remained on the rest of the planet and they'd received fresh reinforcements, so they were finally ready to liberate the Merchant capital, except he still wasn't convinced they had what they needed to succeed. No more resources were available, so he had to find a way through with what they had.

The Ordonians had surrounded the city with trenches and bunkers, filling them with heavy ground-to-ground weaponry along with thousands of soldiers. Anti-air weaponry was set up in the city itself, some of which had already managed to shoot down a few confederate bombers that strayed too close.

To make matters worse, the Imps had acquired Vehlan jamming technology upon making a deal with the Seylins. Since then, they had modified it to jam Vehlan sensors, making it impossible for them to bomb these fortifications from orbit. The trenches and bunkers were far enough away from civilians to make such a strike possible normally, but without sensors there was too high a risk of hitting the city or even their own troops.

Typically, the only way to overcome such an imposing defense was with overwhelming firepower and/or numbers. The attackers had neither. At best, they were evenly matched. Without air cover, they would be slaughtered the moment they tried to move up.

The only option he could see remaining was to demoralize the defenders first, then move in once they'd lost their will to fight. Not an easy task when facing highly trained and experienced Ordonian troops.

6:23 A.M.

"Why haven't we attacked yet?" Private Eric Olian wondered aloud. The attack was supposed to start nearly half an hour ago, yet here they were sitting around doing nothing.

"Don't worry about it. It'll happen when it happens," Private Jeremy Fields responded.

"There has to be something wrong with this long of a delay."

"Like I said, don't worry about it. We saw them moving the tanks around, so I'm sure it's just some last minute adjustments to the plan."

"I suppose you're right."

At that moment, the Vaton artillery cannons behind them opened fire, lighting up the pre-dawn with the brilliant plasma flashes. The soldiers cheered as the bluish plasma orbs sped towards the city, but then fell silent as most of them were destroyed by enemy interceptors.

Another volley.

Same result.

"Looks like this is gonna take a while, folks. Assume defensive positions!" their lieutenant ordered, and the soldiers hustled to obey.

"Told you something was wrong."

"I choose to look at it as a chance to relax and watch the show."

"Shut up."

11:32 A.M.

"Pull them back!" Sam shouted, and Andrie quickly relayed the order.

He'd sent tank formations to attack from all sides under the cover of continuous artillery fire, but it turned out the Ordonians were prepared for that.

The first tanks were destroyed by mines, then soldiers popped out of holes in the ground and opened fire with rocket launchers, damaging or destroying those in the second line when they stopped behind the burning wrecks.

Now enemy tanks were rolling out from the city to finish them off.

The confederate tanks turned and initiated a full retreat, rotating their turrets to fire behind them to avoid getting picked off by their pursuers.

"Target enemy tanks with the artillery!" Sam ordered.

The canons scored several direct hits, forcing the enemy to turn around and return to the city.

"Cease fire," Sam directed, then stepped outside the command post and used a pair of binoculars to survey the scene in the muddy field between him and the city.

He could see a few tanks that were still intact but too damaged to make it out, the crews of which were climbing out. Some of them were shooting at the enemy soldiers now surrounding them, but most had thrown down their weapons and the Ordonians were taking them prisoner.

It was all over less than a minute later when the last of those fighting were killed or realized they were outnumbered and surrendered. The Ordonians then marched their prisoners towards the city and used grenades to scuttle the tanks.

"Resume bombardment schedule," Sam ordered, then left his command post to meet the returning tanks in this sector and check on their crews.

Tuesday, April 20th, 2709
1:07 A.M.

The Ordonian command post entered her view, so Captain Dodge dropped to her belly and began crawling towards it, breathing in the scent of moist ground since as usual she had decided not to wear a helmet. At least it had mostly dried after the rains last week, but she cursed the full moon and clear skies which threatened to reveal her to the enemy. They could use night-vision to see her even if it was darker, but that used power so sentries only used it when they thought they saw something.

As the second day of the siege ended, General Tyquese decided it was time to find out how the imperials were handling the situation. Anxious to do something, Dodge had volunteered. Wanting to learn as much as possible, Tyquese also sent in Scopes and Muddie to infiltrate other locations.

He'd wanted to send Briese as well, but the major wouldn't have it. Their orders from the president were to guard the general, which meant that at least one of them had to stay with him at all times. The general finally had no choice but to let him stay behind.

On her way over, the captain spotted and disabled several landmines, both anti-armor and anti-personnel, clearing the way for their next assault. The bright night made it harder for her to move unseen, but at least it helped her see the mines.

She entered hearing range of the officers in the post, and the first thing she heard was laughter, which was odd for someone who'd been getting shelled for two days straight.

There were no sentries she could see, so she crawled a little closer so as to hear them clearly, then froze in place.

"Two days and those fools haven't even touched our defenses."

"If this is the way they fight a war, this will be over in no time."

"No doubt. This probably won't last even one year, let alone a hundred."

The conversation continued in the same fashion, but by now Dodge had ceased to listen. Given what they were saying, along with the time of night, she concluded they were junior officers. No seasoned soldier would speak this way because they always knew the course of a battle could change in an instant.

However, it was still disconcerting to see the shelling hadn't demoralized them at all. If they were going to break their lines, they first needed to shake them up.

Deciding to take matters into her own hands, Dodge crawled up to the trench to the right of the bunker. She found it empty and pushed forward, falling in then quickly climbing back out the other side.

She lay flat and still for a moment to make sure she hadn't been spotted, then rose to a crouch and proceeded to sneak into the camp set up behind the trench.

It normally required authorization from a commanding officer to change mission parameters, but a comm signal was easily detected and there wasn't time to go back. This was just one of those times she needed to make the decision herself and deal with any consequences later.

The camp itself was lit up, further depriving her of the cover of darkness, but she would find a way.

A patrol turned a corner and headed straight for her, but they were far enough away to not see her in the shadows, especially with her armor's active camouflage engaged, giving her enough time to sidle up to the nearest building and go prone to blend with the ground. Patrols rarely looked down, or up for that matter.

They passed without incident, but the captain stayed where she was for several more seconds to make sure there weren't any others.

Once she was certain it was clear, she climbed the building to get a better view of the camp proper. She looked for any signs of damage from the artillery strikes, but all she saw was several soldiers milling around in small groups, talking and carrying on as if all was normal.

If she was wearing a helmet she could have used its zoom and night-vision systems to get a more detailed look, but as it was she only had her eyes.

One such soldier left the others and headed away from the common areas. She watched him until she was sure of his path, then leapt from building to building until she was right above him.

She jumped and landed in front of him, grabbing his helmet and pulling it off in the process.

Before the soldier could react, she spun on one foot and landed a kick on his left temple, knocking him to the ground after which she jumped on his back and clamped a hand over his mouth while using the other to press a knife to his throat.

"Cooperate or die," she whispered in his ear, and the soldier carefully nodded to signal his compliance.

She pushed him over to a sturdy, narrow-trunked tree clear of the camp, then took his pistol before pushing him away. She covered the prisoner with his own weapon and ordered him to remove his armor. He hesitated, but obeyed when she shifted her aim to his head and stripped to his underarmor, tossing the rest of his equipment on the ground at her feet.

That equipment included a pair of cuffs which she used to secure him to the tree. There was also a cleaning rag which made for the perfect gag.

Now that he was completely incapacitated, she used her knife to carve a message into the tree above his head. It lacked a certain important color, but there was nothing she could do about that so it would have to do as it was.

Finished with him for now, she moved around behind him before silently slipping away.

She found a prefab house on the other side of the camp and snuck around to the back, hoping to find an unguarded door. No such luck.

Moving back to the side, she found an unlocked window, carefully opened it, then climbed through.

She dropped to the floor inside where she remained in a crouch and listened for any patrols. There weren't any, so she located the stairs and moved up to the second floor.

The sound of snoring welcomed her as she exited the stairs, and she couldn't help but smile. This made things a little easier.

She followed the snoring to a bedroom at the end of a hall, then quietly opened the door and slid inside.

Quick and silent, she made her way to the bed and slit its occupant's throat before he had a chance to utter a sound.

His blood pooled on the floor around the bed which she proceeded to dip her knifepoint into, then used it to write something on the wall before leaving.

She made her way back to the tree with the soldier, then brazenly walked in front of him, allowing the moonlight to illuminate her.

She stopped, looked at him, then glanced behind her before returning her gaze to the prisoner.

Next she walked up to him, cleaned her knife on his under-armor, then held it up to shine in the moonlight as if to examine it before returning it to its sheath.

She gave him one last look, then casually walked off into the night.

5:51 A.M.

A commotion outside his tent woke the lieutenant and he groaned as he rolled onto his back and threw an arm across his eyes. Were the confederates really rude enough to attack this early?

He forced himself out of bed, pulled on his armor as quickly as possible, then ran outside while still strapping on his gun belt.

Expecting the excitement to be related to an enemy attack, he was surprised to see soldiers running *away* from the front line. He followed them, shoving his way to the front of a crowd gathered outside the camp, and instantly froze in place.

Directly in front of him was a soldier in nothing but blood-smeared under-armor, gagged and tied to a tree with a star carved into its trunk above his head.

Recovering his wits, the lieutenant ordered someone to cut him loose and for someone else to retrieve the captain.

"Are you injured, soldier?"

"No, sir. The blood isn't mine."

"What happened?"

"I don't know, sir. I was headed to my bunk when someone jumped me from above. Before I knew it, my helmet was off and there was a knife on my throat."

"If the blood isn't yours, where did it come from?"

"I don't know. She just disappeared after tying me up, then a few minutes later, she came back and cleaned her knife on me before disappearing again."

"What makes you think it was a woman?"

"She wasn't wearing a helmet, sir."

"Did you get a good enough look to give a description?"

"I'm not sure. When she came back, I noticed she had red hair, but her face was still mostly in shadow."

A scream pierced the early morning air, interrupting the lieutenant before he could ask his next question.

He rushed towards the source, put on an extra burst of speed when he realized it had come from the captain's house, ran through the door and bounded up the stairs, then pushed people out of his way so he could enter the room.

The lieutenant covered his nose and mouth at the overwhelming metallic odor as he surveyed a room covered in blood and the captain lying on the bed with his throat cut open, then his eyes stopped on the wall to his right.

Written there, in blood, were the words, "We are among you."

6:43 P.M.

Private Olian rested his rifle on a shoulder and trudged back towards the armory.

The Ordonians had launched an attack in an attempt to stop the artillery bombardment, but the confederates managed to fight them off before they could touch a single tank.

Three days down, no telling how many more to go.

"Guess we know how the Imps felt back on Vehla now," Fields commented.

"I don't care how they felt. I'm just ready for this to be over," Olian snapped, growing tired of the other's eternal optimism.

"It'll end. One way or another, it will end."

6:45 P.M.

"Leaving the safety of the city in a long-shot attempt to destroy our canons that ultimately failed. Seems like the beginning of desperation to me," Sam commented as he used a pair of binoculars to watch the defeated imperial troops drag themselves back to their defense perimeter.

"I agree, sir," Breise responded.

He lowered the binoculars and handed them to the major as he turned away, then spotted Captain Dodge silently watching them from the command post entrance.

"Remind me to never get on your bad side," he remarked while ducking through the door.

Wednesday, April 21st, 2709
9:23 A.M.

"Today is the day this battle ends," General Sam Tyquese commented.

The last three days had seen them batter the Ordonian defenses with a near constant artillery barrage, most of which was blocked by interceptor weaponry, but not all.

Enough shots had made it through to cause a decent amount of damage to the fortifications, with one lucky hit even destroying an interceptor gun, allowing them to nearly wipe out the section it was protecting.

The damage wasn't their primary goal, however. Their intent was to wear down the enemy's morale and thus decrease their combat efficiency. The constant shelling, Captain Dodge's impromptu assassination of a senior officer, and a failed counter-attack the previous evening convinced Sam they had achieved that end.

"Send them in."

"Yes, sir," Andrie responded.

The tanks roared with increased power, then surged onto the battlefield behind a screen of drones sweeping the ground with low-powered laser beams which would destroy any remaining mines.

Sniper fire shot out from the trenches and destroyed several drones, but each one that fell was quickly replaced by a fresh one.

Rapid-fire laser guns soon joined the snipers and took out scores of drones, but still they were replaced faster than they could be destroyed and the tanks did not slow their pace.

They finally reached their target position and the drones cleared out as the heavy laser cannons on the Vehlan tanks opened fire. The Ordonian ground canons returned fire, but they were quickly targeted and destroyed before they could do much damage.

"Why aren't they sending out their own tanks?" Colonel Andrie wondered aloud.

"They're too vulnerable to our artillery out in the open, but they'll use them once we make it inside the city," Sam responded.

The general watched through his high-powered binoculars as the tanks blasted apart the trenches, their shields blocking the few rockets that came their way.

He waited until he saw enemy soldiers begin vacating the trenches and take off running for the relative safety of their camps and/or the city beyond, then he ordered the infantry to attack.

Dozens of APCs carrying over a thousand experienced Vehlan soldiers rushed forward on this one side only. The plan was to seize these trenches using overwhelming numbers then spread out and take the rest from within.

The formation continued until it was a few meters behind the tanks where it stopped to off-load the troops.

Soldiers streamed down the ramps, looped around the sides of the vehicles, then ran full-bore towards the trenches. They fired as they went while the tanks continued their own barrage, and the combination effectively suppressed any return fire from the enemy.

Another line of APCs moved into position, this one carrying a mix of Vehlans and Nosines, and Sam ordered them into the fray.

Ordonian domination of this planet was soon to end.

10:11 A.M.

"There!" Eric shouted, pointing at a blast crater to the right.

He ran to it, then dropped to the ground and slid down its side into the trench running through its center, his best friend right beside him.

An enemy on their left swung his rifle towards them but Eric was already aiming in his direction and fired first. He missed and shot the dirt wall instead which sprayed dirt in the soldier's face and blinded him long enough for Jeremy to fire three shots into his torso.

The two of them barely had enough time to stand up before another Ordonian ran out of the opening. Weaponless, he hesitated when he saw them but then he yelled and reached out to grab Eric who stopped him with a rifle butt to the face to send him sprawling into the dirt.

He spun around and grabbed Eric's ankle, but he yanked it from his grasp then shot his opponent. The plasma bolt tore into his shoulder and the man rolled onto his other side screaming, still alive but no longer dangerous.

No more enemies came from this side so he turned around and saw Jeremy struggling with an Ordonian who had grabbed his rifle with both hands and shoved him up against the other side of the crater.

Eric fired twice, the man went limp, and Jeremy shoved him away before regaining his footing and facing his friend.

"I had it handled."

"Sure you did."

The rest of their squad joined them out of the trench to their left, and soon they were moving through the shoulder high ditches, fighting the whole way.

They were *going* to win this.

9:23 P.M.

The general watched from his command center as continuous flashes of light pierced the darkness, showing the intensity of the battle still raging around the city.

It was supposed to be over by now, Sam thought to himself. Yet the defenses were barely halfway secured.

He'd sent in all the soldiers he could, exhausting even their reserves hours ago. They had to be tired, but he couldn't pull any of them back.

"General! Our people are getting pushed back in Sector 5! All other sectors are at a standstill!"

"Enough of this!" Sam responded, then he drew his pistol and ran out of the command center.

"No surrender! No retreat!"

9:27 P.M.

Did he really just do that? Dodge asked herself as she stared after the general.

"What are you waiting for! Charge!" Major Briese yelled as he took off after him.

All those remaining in the command post grabbed their weapons, yelled at the top of their lungs, and took off for the city.

They made it a few meters unchallenged, but then dozens of Deathclouds and Carnages appeared over the city like a swarm of locusts and headed straight for them.

The city's AA batteries had forced the confederates to keep their own airpower on the ground, but when Tyquese saw the incoming craft he stopped running long enough to call them in. They would be protected from the ground weapons as long as they stayed close to the Imps, but it would take them a couple minutes to arrive and the soldiers would be easy prey until then.

The flyers reached them and opened fire with a rain of white plasma, but the impromptu charge hadn't given the soldiers time to get in a proper formation so most of the shots simply hit the ground between them.

"Two o'clock high!" Scopes called out.

Dodge looked up and to her right to see a Carnage headed straight for the general who also saw it and began running back and forth to throw off its aim, but the plane stayed with him.

The other members of the team stopped and opened fire with everything they had, but it wasn't going to be enough.

Wishing Gunney were there, Dodge scanned the area around her for anything she could use and finally spotted a rocket launcher next to a body.

She ran to it, picked it up, and swung back around while bringing it up to aim in the same motion.

The gunship saw only the general and flew straight, granting Dodge all the time she needed to sight it and acquire a lock.

It detected the lock and veered away at the same time she fired, but it was too little too late. The rocket struck a wing and blew it off to send the craft spiraling into the ground where it disappeared in an orange fireball.

A squadron of friendly aircraft arrived on the scene and engaged the enemy, making things safer for the infantry so long as they made sure to avoid anything crashing to the ground.

“Nice shooting,” Scopes commented as Dodge dropped the launcher.
“Where's the general?” she asked.

9:49 P.M.

The trench still occupied by enemy soldiers grew closer and Sam fired towards it as he ran, not accurate enough to hit anything but it was enough to keep the Ordonians down.

He launched himself into the trench and landed on a soldier whom he proceeded to shoot in the chest.

Another one crouched to his right raised his rifle towards him, but Sam dove to his left and the plasma bolt shot over him after which he fired several times. One of the shots struck the man in the face and he fell back onto the ground.

He heard movement behind him and rolled onto his back to see another enemy soldier pointing his rifle at him, but then he was struck by a plasma bolt and collapsed as several confederate soldiers jumped down.

The general pushed himself up, reloaded his pistol, then led the way further into the trench shooting anyone who got in his way.

All seemed to be going well, but then he spotted something up ahead and he dove into an alcove just in time to avoid several plasma shots.

Others weren't as lucky.

At least three of the soldiers with Sam were hit before they could seek cover, one of which fell in front of his hiding spot, so he reached out and pulled him in to discover he was still alive.

“I'm alright, sir,” the soldier reported in a strained tone as Sam examined him. He identified a wound in his side, determined it wasn't immediately serious, so he applied a bandage and returned his attention to the fight.

The trench was filled with plasma bolts, both the white of the Ordonians and the light blue of the Vaton weapons the confederates were using.

They couldn't advance through that, and anyone who tried wouldn't live long enough to regret his stupidity.

It was possible for them to climb out and attempt to approach the enemy position on the ground above, but that would leave them too exposed.

He could think of only one other option.

"Grenades!" he shouted as he pulled out one of his own and primed it.

He leaned against the side of his alcove opposite the enemy position, judged the distance the best he could, then threw the grenade and dove onto the wounded soldier to cover him.

The explosion came, quickly followed by a second, then three more. Debris rained down on them, none of it larger than a small stone.

Sam jumped to his feet, yelled for his soldiers to follow him, then vacated his cover and ran towards the enemy position which he could now see was a small bunker.

They made it inside without incident, but then an enemy grabbed him and pushed him towards a wall, but they tripped over something and fell to the ground. Sam used the momentum of the fall to throw the soldier over his head and into the wall where he slid down to the floor.

Both of them quickly stood up and squared off, but then the Ordonian saw he was alone and outnumbered so he raised his hands in surrender.

Two confederates restrained him while Sam relaxed his pose and looked around, discovering it was a dead body he had tripped over.

"Secure the bunker and get our flag up top," he ordered. His soldiers obeyed and he went to take a look out the other door.

There were no enemies in the immediate vicinity, but he could see the flashes of weapons fire further down. Those that should have been there must have been called in to reinforce another position.

He turned back and was about to give the order to push forward when he saw two flashbangs come sailing through the first door which went off before he could shout a warning.

Blind and deaf, he threw himself to the ground in an attempt to wait it out long enough to fight back, but it was to no avail.

The moment his senses started to clear, he was hauled to his feet and made to face someone, his blurry vision slowly clearing to reveal a fully armored Star Knight Captain.

"The confederacy's true weakness becomes apparent when a general is required to take to the field of battle," the knight captain taunted.

"We must have frightened the empire somehow if it feels the need to send knights into a common battle."

"Our presence has nothing to do with your attack. We are stationed here as overseers and were here before you showed up."

"Oh, so you're just out here sightseeing then?" Sam remarked. He stood no chance against five Star Knights, or even just one if he was being honest, so his best option was to stall for time.

"Precisely."

"See anything good?"

"I've seen better," the captain answered.

A sarcastic comment was on the tip of Sam's tongue, but he was interrupted by the knights guarding the doors reporting movement outside.

The knight captain started to reply, but Sam took advantage of the distraction by grabbing his weapon with one hand and punching him with the other. His opponent was wearing a helmet, but Sam was wearing armored gloves, so it was still a solid blow.

Seemingly unaffected, the captain backhanded the general which sent him sprawling onto the floor.

Two shots rang out and one door guard fell but the second managed to dive out of the way and escape harm.

When the captain turned to look that way, Sam grabbed his ankles and pulled, causing him to fall forward at which point he went to jump on his back, but an elbow to his face deflected him to the side.

He landed on his back where he found himself pinned when his opponent climbed on top of him and squeezed his torso between his knees.

The captain drew his knife and went to stab it into Sam's chest, but he blocked the arm with his own.

Instead of trying to force his way through, the knight pulled the knife to the side, slashing Sam's arm in the process. When he pulled that arm back, the knight slashed the other one.

Now that the arms were out of the way, he tried to stab him in the chest again, but Sam kneed him in the buttox, pushing him forward and off.

He rolled onto his stomach and pushed up into a crouch, ready to defend himself again, but this time someone else was already engaging the knight.

The newcomer landed a series of successive blows culminating in a punch to the face powerful enough to crack the face shield and knock the knight to the ground where he stayed this time.

His rescuer turned to face him as he got back on his feet, allowing him to see it was Major Briese since for some reason these guardians preferred not to wear helmets.

"Guess it's a good thing my brother assigned you to protect me after all."

"I'm inclined to agree," the major responded, then pointed at the general's arms, "You're injured."

"So are you," Sam responded, pointing to a patch of blood on the major's lower right side.

"I'll live."

“So will I. How are the others?”

“We're all a little banged up, but Scopes is pretty bad. Muddie's working on him now,” Captain Dodge answered.

Concerned, Briese and Tyquese walked over to where the medic was working on their fallen teammate, who was unconscious and covered in blood.

“How bad is he?” Sam questioned.

“Pretty bad. At least one gunshot and multiple knife wounds.”

At this point, a few more confederate soldiers showed up, one of whom turned out to be Colonel Andrie.

The general left the medic to his work and the other two guardians to check each other's wounds and took Andrie aside to ask for a report.

“The outer defenses are under our control. We're moving in supplies now, and I've taken the liberty of pulling in more troops from the rest of the planet. Once they get here, they'll take over in the trenches while those involved in the fighting return to base.”

“No. Secure and regroup, but no one is returning to base. There's still work to be done.”

“You're not suggesting we push forward into the city!”

“No, I'm *not* suggesting it. I'm ordering it. We give the enemy no time to breathe,” Sam insisted, then noticed the knight captain stirring.

He hauled the man to his feet then shoved him against a wall and got right in his face.

“Tell me everything about your defenses inside the city. Troop count, fortified positions, everything,” he hissed, but the knight's only reaction was to laugh in his face.

“I am a Star Knight, an elite warrior sworn to serve the emperor. I'm not going to tell you anything.”

“I may not scare you, but what about my friends here? In case you didn't notice, they're Azul Guardians, more than a match for any knight. You should also know that because of you, a member of their team is dying. Tell me what I want to know, or I turn you over to them.”

A trace of fear entered the knight's eyes as he glanced at the guardians, but it quickly disappeared behind stubborn resolve as he stared into Sam's eyes once again.

"I have been trained to resist all forms of torture."

"Have it your way," Sam responded, then pushed the knight towards Major Briese and Captain Dodge.

"I don't care what you do. Just get me the information I want," he told them.

Captain Dodge pointed her rifle at the knight's head and ordered him to remove his armor, but Major Briese pulled the general away.

"We could torture him for days before getting anything out of him," he whispered.

"You have until our reinforcements arrive. If you don't get anything, so be it, but I want you to try anyway."

The major studied him with a note of concern in his tired eyes, and Sam stared back, briefly wondering if the man could somehow see his face behind his helmet's faceplate.

They stayed this way for several seconds, but then the major finally turned away and helped Dodge drag the knight into the bunker's darkest corner.

Thursday, April 22nd, 2709
6:21 A.M.

A nearby retaining wall proved too inviting and Eric half-collapsed against it where he was soon joined by Jeremy who for once didn't attempt an optimistic remark.

"I feel like I've fought and killed a thousand people single-handedly," Eric commented.

"Me too."

The sounds of battle could still be heard around the city, but for the moment, the immediate area was quiet, allowing the two friends a moment to catch their breath and survey the scene around them.

Both directions of the street in front of them were littered with the bodies of both confederate and imperial soldiers, none of them moving since the wounded had already been carried off.

The street itself was filled with craters and covered with rubble, rendering it unrecognizable. There were a few vehicles, some now wrecks, but for the most part it was empty.

"Sun's coming up," Jeremy observed, and Eric looked up to see the first rays of light coming over the buildings, accentuated by columns of smoke.

"This is General Tyquese to all units. Cease fire immediately. The Ordonians have surrendered," the general's voice came over their comms.

Before the two friends could react to the news, a group of five enemy soldiers came out of a building further up the street. Despite the news of the surrender, Eric and Jeremy pushed away from the wall and readied themselves for a fight.

Their movement attracted the attention of the imperials, who proceeded to put their weapons on the ground and walk towards them with their hands in the air.

"Well, guess it's time to get back to work," Eric observed.

"Our shift does start in about half an hour. Might as well go in early and get a little extra done."

"You go in early if you want to. I'm getting breakfast."

"Come on, early bird gets the worm, or worms in this case."

"I suppose you're right. Let's go get 'em."

OES Lentaise Four
7:00 A.M.

His muscles burning in protest, Canza forced himself to lift the weights one last time, then he slowly dropped his arms until he could lean over and place the dumbbells on the floor.

He was covered in sweat, but his breathing remained steady as he rested and looked around the gym.

This was one of his favorite things to do, not merely as a means of maintaining and improving his health but because it gave him the opportunity to be around his fellow soldiers without his rank coming between them.

In here, there were no ranks. They were simply people, working to better their bodies and minds.

No matter what his position may be, Max felt as though he were one of them. Each and every one of them sought to protect and advance the empire's interests. Out in the rest of the world, his position forced him to stand apart, but here he could enjoy their company as he pleased.

As he was dwelling on these things, Secondary Zenzal entered the room, glanced around until he saw the primary, then approached him.

"We've lost the Merchant's capital," he reported simply.

"Order any remaining space forces out of the Merchant's Interest. Ground forces are to remain and resist the confederate invasion as long as possible," Canza ordered.

"Why not pull them all out, keep them all in, or send reinforcements for that matter?"

"It would be a waste of resources to send reinforcements and the spacecraft we have left in the region are too few to be of any use. When the confederacy is forced to attack our ground forces, they will be the ones wasting resources. By the time the fighting is over, the Merchant's economy will be wrecked and therefore useless to them."

"That's still sacrificing a lot of lives, sir."

“Sacrifice is a part of war, and it is up to us as leaders to know when it is necessary. We cannot allow the confederacy to gain control of the Merchant economy as it currently exists,” Canza responded, looking deep into his subordinate's eyes as he did so.

With the secondary's history of disobeying orders because of conflict with his personal views or assessments, it occurred to Canza that he might disobey this one and he could see in his eyes that he was considering the idea.

All the reasons he gave for the order were true, but he also wanted to test the man. He had to know his limits if he was to be fully trusted with their project.

“Order confirmed,” Zenzal finally said, but he didn't leave.

“Is there something else?”

“I think we need to discuss why you brought me here. I can't stay much longer,” the secondary admitted.

“I agree,” Canza responded, then stood, put his weights back in the rack, then led the way to a deserted corner of the room as he took a deep drink of water from a bottle.

The primary set his water bottle next to a leg press machine then used his palco to scan for surveillance devices under the guise of checking his workout stats, but he didn't find anything so he sat on the machine and used it while Zenzal stood to his right and kept an eye on the room while they talked.

“We must find a way to ensure continuity of government should the emperor become a liability,” Canza proposed.

“I'm more concerned with the emperor himself. If his removal becomes necessary, we need a plan for that.”

“The legionnaires provide us with the edge we need to ensure our success and I'm in the process of preparing them, but we'll need political allies to pull this off, starting with the governors.”

“All the governors are loyal to the emperor.”

"No one is without weakness, so all we have to do is learn theirs and use it to ensure their cooperation when the time comes. However, if either of us begins investigating towards that end we will be discovered and stopped," Canza warned.

"We are still the only ones who know about my mercenaries, so they remain outside any scrutiny and can investigate without raising suspicion. Even if they are caught and reveal they're working for me, I can deny their claims and it will be the word of criminals against mine," Zenzal inferred.

"The confederacy has also managed to nearly eliminate them, making them ever more useless in their current assignment. Task those that are left with investigating the governors, then use what they find to intimidate them and bring them to our side. I'll send you a list of some likely candidates to get you started. Once you receive it, return to Ordeos," Canza confirmed.

"Yes, sir," Zenzal saluted, then left.

Halting his exercise, Max looked at the soldiers hard at work lifting weights and running on treadmills.

The path he was walking could easily lead to civil war. Many of those he was now looking at would probably die in that war, if not all of them.

Part of him wondered if he was betraying them.

Yet his resolve remained. He had to do what was best for the empire, even if it meant risking the worst.

Chapter Ten
Lost Guardians

Tikas
Saturday, March 24th, 2709
7:51 P.M.

The setting sun cast an eerie glow over the ruins as Private Exodus looked on, unable to see much of them through the trees but the image he saw from a distance during their landing was still fresh in his mind, leaving him to wonder if the cities of his home planet Swarnlia would meet the same fate.

Tikas was the homeworld of a thriving, independent nation at the start of recorded history, but that was before the Ordeon Empire laid claim to its territory and invaded.

The Tikans fought back hard, but were eventually defeated. As a warning to the planet's inhabitants, as well as everyone else, the Ordonians forbade the rebuilding of cities destroyed in the fighting, the ruins of which persisted to this day.

It was in one of those ruined cities where Exodus and the majority of his team were hiding while a scouting party gathered intel.

There were no longer any streets, or paved areas of any kind. A few skyscrapers still reached into the air, but most were bombed out and looted long ago. Grass and vines covered everything, and several buildings were nearly obscured by trees. Surely every last vestige of human habitation would have disappeared long ago if not for the empire maintaining it as a "historic site".

The sun finally disappeared below the horizon, and the local insects struck up their chorus. Some birds joined in as well, their calls echoing in the empty buildings to add a ghostly ambiance to the scene.

"This is why we fight," Sergeant Lacey commented from his right.

"I'm sure the Imps would say this happened *because* the people fought."

"The people wouldn't have needed to fight if the Ordonians had left them alone. This destruction is the result of people taking that which is not theirs."

"Who decides what belongs to who?"

The sergeant didn't say anything and Exodus wondered if she would answer the question, but then Lacey spoke up again.

"I don't have an answer for that. I would say something belongs to you if you work for it, fight for it, and improve it. The empire is doing all these things on the Vehlan planets, yet those planets do not belong to them."

"Why don't you two stop being philosophical and come get something to eat?" Captain Ontier interrupted.

"Yes, sir," the two responded simultaneously, but a noise coming from outside their campsite stopped them.

They listened closely and determined it to be something moving through the tall grass towards them so they each raised a weapon in response.

The sound moved closer, and fingers tightened around triggers.

Rubble from the small building they occupied kept the grass from getting too thick around the building itself, preventing anything from getting to them undetected. Still, if something came running out of that grass they would have mere seconds to respond.

Exodus spotted some of the blades moving and trained his rifle in their direction.

A hand reached out and pushed the grass aside to allow a plainclothes man to step through, who saw the weapons pointed at him and threw his hands into the air.

"Stand down!" Ontier ordered, and the other two relaxed to point their rifles at the ground. The man was the leader of their scouting party, the rest of which soon stepped out behind him.

"Feeling a little jumpy tonight?" the scout leader, Lieutenant Fathison, quipped.

"We're on an enemy planet. What do you expect?" Lacey responded.

"We're in the middle of nowhere on an enemy planet. Try relaxing a little."

"You try following procedure and calling ahead."

"Enough! Report in, Lieutenant," Ontier ended the dispute.

"We tracked down the aliases for each of the Guardian team members on mission here. Their cover is intact, and they are still working at the primary target."

"Why haven't they pulled out?" Lacey wondered aloud.

"Exodus, why didn't the team you were with pull out?" Ontier questioned.

"We were cut off for over a year, and good information was hard to come by. We didn't even know the war was over until several days later, so as far as we knew, we were still doing our duty."

"That can't be the case here. These guys have to know the war is over," Lacey observed.

"The most likely reason is they can't leave, at least not without fighting their way out. They signed a five-year contract with the officer's academy for their cover and they are boarded on the campus. Attempting to leave would blow their cover," Ontier revealed.

"And that academy is a fortress. Nobody gets in or out without being carded," Fathison commented.

"Did you get a look at it?"

"Affirmative. Getting our people out is not going to be easy, but I think we have an idea."

"Let's hear it," Ontier responded, then took a seat near the hotplate while the others gathered around.

Monday, April 26th, 2709
12:23 A.M.

Lightning split the sky, briefly illuminating the soldiers crouched near the storm drain exit. Thunder followed, shaking the ground and rattling the grate with its ferocity.

Looking up at the sky, Exodus saw only blackness, at least until another flash lit up the thick clouds.

"Captain, I think we should pull back. If this storm lets loose while we're in the tunnels, we'll drown," Sergeant Lacey commented.

"Negative. Fathison got his hands on a weather report saying this system will last for at least a week. We don't have enough supplies to hold out that long. We go in now," Ontier refused.

The team's only way into the facility where the Guardian's team was working undercover was through a series of storm drains that emptied outside the complex itself. The area experienced storms frequently enough that the drains were large enough to move through, but while that gained them a way inside, it also came with increased risk at the moment.

"In position," Lieutenant Fathison reported via comlink. He was leading half their team in through another drain exit on the opposite side of the facility.

"Alright, move in. Make it fast, there's no telling how long we have," Ontier responded, then signaled for Lacey to begin.

They had already disabled the detection grid by setting up a feedback loop, so she pulled out a plasma cutter and got to work opening a hole in the grate.

As she cut, the others moved in around her to mask any excess light coming from the cutter. It was designed to emit as little light as possible, and the area should be deserted, but it was best not to take any chances.

The thin material presented no challenge, and the team was inside less than a minute later.

Even underground, they could still hear the thunder rumbling above them, encouraging them to keep up the pace.

They kept going until Ontier signaled a halt under a grate in the ceiling. The team took up defensive positions while he used a periscope device to scout the area above them.

"Clear," he finally whispered, and the sergeant climbed the ladder on the wall, removed the grate and exited first. The two privates followed, and last came the corporal and captain.

"That house is our target. Move in," Ontier pointed, and Lacey led the way across the street into the yard.

"I don't like this, Captain. It's too quiet," the corporal whispered when they were reassembled behind a bush.

"They're not expecting any trouble."

"From what I know of Imps, they would keep all possible entrances to a place like this guarded, even the sewers."

"You're thinking too much," Ontier concluded, then comlinked Fathison for a status report.

"Approaching target now, sir. All clear so far."

"Good. Move in when ready."

The captain signaled for silence then led the way to the back door which he found to be unlocked so he quietly swung it open to allow Lacey inside, rifle at the ready. Since they were in the middle of a fortified military academy it wasn't surprising most people would keep their doors unlocked.

"Execute Plan A."

With Privates Exodus and Gant following, the corporal found the stairs and led the way to the second floor while Lacey and Ontier swept the bottom floor.

Moving quickly and silently, they checked every single room. Lightning continued to flash outside, periodically lighting up the inside and exposing the soldiers, but they managed to get through the entire house without any trouble.

"First floor clear."

"Second floor clear."

"There's nobody here?"

"Fathison, report!"

"Bunkhouse empty, sir. No activity of any kind."

"So what do we do now? Search the entire base!"

As the team digested their change of circumstance, the rain finally started outside. It was light, but that was likely to change soon and then their exit would be cut off.

Floodlights suddenly snapped on outside, bathing the entire house in light and the soldiers' face shields automatically tinted to protect their vision.

Reacting instinctively, each one made for the nearest window and took cover at its side where they could see out. What they saw was not encouraging.

From his position, Exodus saw two combat jeeps, five Star Knights, and at least ten soldiers.

"This is Knight Captain Crain to Confederate intruders! You are surrounded with no hope of escape! Surrender now, or be killed!"

The soldiers offered no response.

"What do we do, Captain?" Lacey whispered via comlink.

"Fathison, are you also surrounded?"

"Affirmative."

"We know you are in there! Silence will not help you now!" Crain challenged.

Still no response from the team.

"I can see you need some convincing!" Crain shouted, then stepped aside as a pair of knights dragged a man in brown prison clothes out of the shadows and tossed him to the ground.

"This man is the last of those you for whom you came! The others are all dead! Surrender now, and his life will be spared along with yours!"

Again, the soldiers stayed silent.

Exodus looked away long enough to check on the others in the room with him. The corporal was tapping his thumb on his weapon and keeping a laser focus out the window while Gant was looking around nervously as if for an escape. He spotted Exodus looking at him and snapped his attention back to the window.

"So be it. Your friend's life is now forfeit," Crain stated, then aimed a pistol at his prisoner.

Exodus and the corporal both raised their weapons to firing position, but they were saved from intervening.

Before the knight could fire, his prisoner rolled towards him and tripped him then jumped atop him where he proceeded to beat at his unprotected face with bound hands.

The soldiers in the house opened fire and sent the other imperials running for cover, preventing them from helping their superior.

Once in cover, they returned fire and clouds of steam began to fill the area between the combatants as their plasma bolts vaporized the thickening rain.

The guardian continued battering the knight, but then he went limp and Crain pushed him off.

The knight rose to his feet, casually cleaned a knife on the dead prisoner's clothes then returned it to its sheath, seemingly oblivious to the firefight taking place around him.

He then reached out to each side and slowly rotated in place to call for a cease fire, ignoring the rain and the blood flowing from his nose even as it stained his grey uniform.

Both sides stopped shooting, and he stopped to face the house once more.

"You choose death over everything the empire offers! So be it!" he observed, then turned back towards his men.

"*Burn it!*"

The Ordonians opened up with everything they had, but ignored the soldiers and targeted the house itself. The plasma bolts quickly evaporated the water covering the house and ignited blazes in its place.

The team returned fire, but to little effect. They could barely see through the steam and smoke rising around them and the spreading fires would soon burn them alive.

"Grenade!" Gant called out as one came flying through his window.

Exodus managed to dive into a corner and cover his head with both hands before it went off to blast him with a wave of heat.

He rolled over and discovered the room engulfed in flames through which he was barely able to see his unmoving companions. He rushed over to them, skirting the flames and nearly slipping on the floor now wet from the rain pouring in through the busted windows, but there was nothing he could do for them.

Both were dead.

With the fire growing around him, he had no time to give in to shock. Instead, gut-shredding fear rose within him and he ran from the room.

Giving no thought to the enemy soldiers still surrounding the building, or the fact he was on the second floor, he ran full speed and crashed through a window on the other side of the house.

He landed on a bush and rolled off it to come to a stop beside a stunned enemy soldier.

His heart beating faster than he ever thought possible, Exodus jumped to his feet, grabbed his opponent's rifle away from him, then swung it at his head.

The soldier fell into the bush and Exodus spun the rifle around and shot him in the back before he could recover.

Not waiting to see if there were any others, the private took off running as fast as he could.

He got at least a mile away before collapsing behind a random building.

His energy used up, he lay there facedown trying to catch his breath, but then he felt a hand on his shoulder.

Extra adrenaline flooded his system and he spun around with rifle pointed up only to have it yanked out of his grip. He reached for his sidearm, but his opponent kicked his hand aside before reaching down and grabbing him by the front of his armor.

"Snap out of it, Exodus! It's me!"

Finally stopping to take a good look at his "attacker", he recognized Sergeant Lacey and stopped struggling. When he calmed down, the sergeant let him go and returned his rifle, which was actually the one he took from the imperial.

"What happened to your weapon, Private?"

"I must have dropped it when the grenade went off. Did anyone else get out?"

"Nobody from our half of the team, but I managed to get Fathison on the comlink. He escaped the ambush at his location, but he's the only one."

"What about the captain?" Exodus asked, and Lacey could only respond by looking down and shaking her head.

Over half of their team, dead. Their team leader, dead. And they were still stuck in enemy territory.

"Now what?"

Tikas
Academy Spaceport
8:04 A.M.

"What are we going to do?" Exodus questioned.

"There's no way out of here. They have the whole place locked down tight," Lacey observed.

There was no way for the surviving team members to exit the campus, especially since the storm drains were now flooded, so they had made their way to the small spaceport on the facility grounds where they found an empty hangar as the sun was coming up. The worst of the storm had passed for now, but a steady drizzle continued to fall from an overcast sky, mingling the smell of wet dirt and pavement with that of thruster exhaust.

At least their armor was more waterproof than it was bulletproof, but staying dry did little to ease their misery.

The three of them were currently crouched in the shadows near the main door watching as the day's activities got under way.

From this vantage point, they were able to see several Star Knights, some patrolling the grounds while the rest stood guard at the entrances to all the ships. Clearly they knew there were survivors of last night's ambush and sought to block their escape.

"We are not going to surrender. We will find a way out," Lieutenant Fathison encouraged.

Exodus couldn't help but think he'd been in this situation before, with another team. Except that time it was a civilian spaceport and no one was actively hunting them.

He took another look outside and saw that none of the cargo compartments were guarded.

"This Vaton armor has an independent air supply, right?"

"About two hours worth, why?" Fathison answered.

"The knights aren't guarding the cargo bays, so we should sneak into one of them."

"We'll never get that far unnoticed," Fathison argued.

"So we grab a few port workers and steal their uniforms. Then we load the armor into crates and put them back on after we're onboard," Lacey suggested, but then added, "Only problem is, two hours isn't long enough to get us anywhere."

"We wait until the ship enters hyperspace, then we force our way into the cabin and take it over," Fathison proposed.

The three of them looked at each other as if expecting someone to bring up another objection, but no one said a thing.

They had a plan.

1:43 P.M.

The cargo transport had launched nearly an hour ago, giving it more than enough time to break orbit and enter hyperspace.

Since using the helmet comlinks carried the risk of being detected, Fathison used hand-signals to order Lacey to the left side of the airlock leading to the passenger compartment while he took the right. Exodus took up a crouching position several feet in front and took aim with his rifle just in case someone was on the other side.

The lieutenant pulled out a small computer, attached it to the keypad and activated it. Numbers flashed on the pad's display then stopped in a four-digit configuration.

Several seconds passed with nothing happening, but then the door slid up to reveal an empty room barely large enough to hold the three of them.

Fathison went through first, followed by Lacey, and finally Exodus squeezed himself into what space remained. Putting the computer on the keypad in this room, Fathison repeated the process.

The door behind them slid shut, air rushed into the room, and then the next door opened.

Exiting quickly, each team member took a knee in the EVA prep room on the other side, but it was empty.

They left the room and made their way to the bridge, checking every corner on the way, but this soon after launch the crew was still at their stations.

"Hands in the air!" Fathison shouted as he burst onto the bridge, the other two right behind him.

Six crew members, standard for this type of vessel, spun to face him, the surprise plain on their faces.

"Is this a joke?" the captain questioned, but then he recognized the armor, saw the weapons pointed at him and his crew and quickly threw his hands into the air. The rest followed suit.

"No joke, Captain. This ship is now ours. Do as we say and you will live. Resist, and we will space you."

The crew's only reaction was to look at their captors with sheer terror. Exodus doubted the lieutenant would actually space anyone, but he wasn't about to tell them that.

"Good, now everyone but the captain line up between my two friends here. As for you, you're going to set a new course, then open a comlink," Fathison ordered.

Revenue Central
4:52 P.M.

Word came to Major Briese that there was a call for him from the president while he was working in his temporary office, so he passed his work into the background of his mobile computer and told the communications officer to put it through. He could use his palco for both the work and the call, but this computer allowed for the use of both hands which was more comfortable when working long periods of time.

"I have some bad news, Major. The team I assigned to locate more Azul Guardians was ambushed while following their first lead. Only three managed to escape and report in. They did manage to find out that the guardians they were looking for were all executed."

"Private Exodus?"

"He is among the survivors."

The major took a moment to catch his breath, mourning all those lost. He felt sorrow for all of them, but the loss of the guardians hurt the most. There were so few of them left and every death pushed them that much closer to extinction.

"What happened?"

"We don't know how, but the Star Knights discovered the identity of undercover guardians and captured them, then set an ambush for anyone who came looking for them."

"Star Knights were there?"

"Yes."

"With all due respect, Mr. President, this is precisely why my team should be handling this. We are the only ones qualified to go up against the knights."

"I understand that, Major, but the events on Merchanta only reinforce my belief that you are exactly where you are needed. The general would probably be dead right now if it wasn't for you. However, I am willing to let you choose the members of the new team. That way, you can find those who stand the best chance of resisting the knights after you and your team," Tyquese offered.

The major considered pressing his argument, but realized it would do no good. The president was right.

"Very well, sir. I'll get on it right away."

"Before I go, how is Lieutenant Suese doing?"

"If Specialist Nafais hadn't been on hand to stop the bleeding as quickly as he did, we would have lost him right away. The gunshot wound proved severe and nearly finished him off, but Nafais was able to stabilize him long enough to get him to the hospital ship. All indications are that he will make a full recovery, but he will be out of commission for a while."

"Good news. We need as much of that as we can get. Carry on, Major."

Revenue Central Outskirts
6:23 P.M.

"I've got it!" Sam called out. The ball fell neatly into his hands, and he continued running without missing a beat.

An opposing team member moved in to tackle him, but he darted to the left, causing the man to fly past him.

Then another unseen opponent impacted his side, knocking him to the ground. He claimed the ball for himself, then took off in the other direction.

"Not so fast!" Sam declared as he jumped to his feet and engaged a pursuit course.

There were no pauses in this game unless someone scored or a time-out was called. If the other team had the ball, your job was to get it away from them. When your side had it, the objective was to get it to the goal line, either by running it or by passing it between teammates.

The man Sam was chasing tossed the ball to a nearby mate, who then passed it to another one further down the field.

No sooner was the ball caught than that person was tackled and the ball recovered by Sam's team.

Already running towards his goal, Sam declared himself open. An opponent attempted to intercept the pass, but he jumped and caught it in the air.

Nearby teammates then kept anyone from tackling him long enough for him to score. Cheers erupted from the sidelines as he spiked the ball and shouted in victory.

"You're pretty good at this," someone said from behind him, and he turned to see Major Briese watching him with an amused smile.

"I played all through high-school and my one year of college. Wanted to make it a career, but was pressured into joining the military," Sam explained. He stepped to the sideline and signaled someone to take his place so he could take a break, then he grabbed a cold beer out of a cooler and took a long drink.

Things had stayed quiet since their liberation of the Merchant capital, so he'd decided it was time for everyone to blow off a little steam. He'd given half of their forces on this planet two days off, after which they would return to duty and give the other half a couple days of free time.

Here at the capital the sun was shining and the weather was warm, making it the perfect time for a ballgame.

"I bet you never played against Nosines back then. That has to change things up," Briese commented.

"It makes things interesting, that's for sure. They can't go very fast without tripping, but their strength more than makes up for it. I watched one drag two guys for several feet before a third was finally able to take him down," Sam described, then asked, "So, what is it you want to tell me?"

"I received confirmation on the deaths of more Azul Guardians. The team sent to extract them was nearly wiped out discovering even that much."

"There are more of you out there. I have no doubts about that."

"How can you be so sure?"

"We are still finding regulars that have been in hiding for years. If they've managed to hide this long, both from the empire and us, then it stands to reason that special forces units will hold out even longer," Sam explained. The major's only response was to nod thoughtfully.

"In the meantime, maybe you should consider training some new recruits. The Nosines would be a good place to start."

"The Nosines?"

"You said it yourself. They are a new element that changes things up considerably," Sam suggested.

"Their strength might give us an edge over the Star Knights," Briese considered as he watched the game.

Chapter Eleven
Cost of Defiance

OES Lentaise Four
Wednesday, April 28th, 2709
7:58 A.M.

"Wave one, commence," Primary Canza ordered, then watched the tactical screen as the first wave of his attack dropped out of hyperspace and immediately opened fire on the Vaton defenders, beginning their invasion of the second conglomerate planetary system.

The defenders instantly returned fire which showed they somehow knew about the attack beforehand and had armed their systems to deny the Ordonians any early advantage.

The ease with which they had taken the border was clearly due to the Vatons choosing to consolidate their resources in the systems themselves where they had a greater homefield advantage.

To monitor the reactions of the personnel aboard his ships engaged in the battle, Canza had ordered comlinks established with all of them. This particular strategy required a certain knowledge of the mood of those fighting, an aspect of battle not conveyed by any screen. These links relayed everything that was said on the bridge of each vessel straight to him.

"Taking fire!"

"Enemy has received minimal damage!"

"They were expecting us!"

"Fire all batteries!"

"Fighter wings to interception duties!"

The primary could feel everyone's eyes on him, waiting for his next order. How long was he going to leave his people without support? Did he plan to sacrifice them?

He ignored them and continued to hold off on sending in the second wave.

"There's too many of them!"

"This isn't working!"

"Defense Formation Seven!" the wave commander finally ordered and their ships tightened up with the smaller ones surrounding the capitols.

A move from offense to defense made them appear weak, seemingly making them an easy target.

The Vatons did not take the bait.

The plan was for them to sense an easy kill and surround the first wave with overwhelming firepower after which the rest of Canza's fleet would surround them and destroy them in a crossfire, but they stayed in position using necessary force only.

"A smart enemy," Knight Ricine commented tauntingly, but he ignored her.

"Second wave. Execute Plan Beta," he ordered. Nearly half of the remaining fleet dropped out of hyperspace and joined the action, but not all at once.

Each squadron entered the battlefield separately and in a different location in an attempt to force the defenders to scramble to divert resources against them, thus setting them off-balance.

Yet once again, the Vatons proved a capable adversary, denying their enemy the hoped-for results. Their coordination proved flawless, and the core of their defense remained unaffected.

The effect on the Ordonian crews was immediate.

"Strike ineffective!"

"Enemy formation unaltered!"

"Hull breach! Deck eleven!"

"Taking heavy losses!"

"First fighter wave almost depleted!"

"Any damage to enemy!?"

"Negligible, sir!"

Ricine's voice rose above the chatter to say, "These people will make a great addition to the empire should that ever happen."

Smiling, Canza turned to Tactical and ordered, "Take us in."

"Yes, sir. Executing Plan Gamma."

All remaining Ordonian ships, including the Lentaise Four, dropped out of hyperspace in the exact middle of the enemy fleet. A dangerous move since the exiting ships could slam into those already in normal space, destroying both, but imperial technology proved itself once again and all ships arrived safely.

The defenders weren't as lucky.

Spatial distortions present at the opening of any hyperspace window ripped into the nearest Vaton ships and tore them apart.

Wasting no time, the new arrivals opened fire on the survivors, soon creating a hole in the middle of their fleet. Once the center was gone, the perimeter began to collapse as well.

At this point there was no stopping the attackers, but the Vatons fought on anyway, inflicting as much damage as possible before succumbing. Some of them even rammed the closest imperial ships, while the rest either self-destructed or were destroyed.

"Why self-destruct?" Tactical wondered out loud.

"They think their technology is better than ours and want to prevent us from stealing it," Canza responded.

"Fools," Tactical remarked as the last Vaton ship self-destructed.

"They may put up a good fight, but everyone falls before us," Canza remarked as the fleet moved to take up position around each inhabited world.

"I'd rather not wait another hundred years to end *this* war," Ricine responded, determined to have the last word.

"Orbits achieved," the ship's captain reported.

"Commence bombardment," Canza ordered.

Instead of conducting a ground invasion, the primary had opted to bomb this system into submission. Their targets were all military bases, police centers, and fire stations along with a few farms and food warehouses. The food supply would not be destroyed, but it would be depleted enough to where they would run out within a few weeks without outside support.

Hospitals would remain untouched for now, but they would be destroyed as well if the population didn't surrender.

"Communication incoming from the emperor, sir."

"I'll take it in my office. Knight Ricine, you have command," Canza responded, then took off for his office.

"Your Majesty?" he greeted once the connection was made.

"The Vatons are displaying a proclivity for warfare one wouldn't expect from a nation claiming its sole purpose to be the advancement of science, but you reminded them that Ordonian ability remains greater than all others," Lentaise commented.

"They can slow us down, but they will never stop us. Do you have new orders for me?"

"Yes. It is time to widen our offensive."

"That could spread our forces too thin."

"Our decision not to defend the Merchant's Interest has left us with more than enough resources."

"Those resources are best utilized ensuring the safety of our home territories. It is only a matter of time before the confederacy launches an invasion with the goal of reaching Ordeos itself."

"You are eliminating their ability to produce new weapons, and this invasion will cut off the supplies they need to build new ships rendering them unable to launch an attack such as you describe. This is our best chance for a decisive victory and it is what we are going to do."

"As you wish, Majesty."

Amberlis Territories (Border)
Friday, April 30th, 2709
9:57 A.M.

"Finally, some action," Private Menza muttered as he took his place in formation on the troop carrier's hangar deck.

"Quiet!" his corporal hissed.

After weeks of patrolling within the former union territories, Menza and his fellow soldiers were all itching for a fight. Secondary Zenzal originally placed them there to put down any uprisings initiated by the recently conquered populations, but none had appeared, leaving them without an enemy to fight.

That was all about to change.

"Listen carefully, soldiers, as this is not your standard mission. Our mission is to conduct guerrilla raids against the Amberlis Territories in preparation for a full invasion. We will begin by disrupting their supply shipments to the confederacy," the lieutenant briefed them.

"Isn't that more of a job for the special forces or the star knights?" someone in the formation blurted out.

"The emperor has not ordered the knights to do this, and Primary Canza has chosen us, not the special forces. Any other questions?" the lieutenant responded, snidely twisting the word 'questions'.

The room was silent.

"Our first target is a shipping facility on the border world Witt. A squadron of capital ships will keep the orbital defenses busy while a wing of bombers takes out any anti-air defenses on the ground.

"Your job is to go in after the bombers and secure the warehouses. Another team will load our transports with the processed minerals stored inside before exfil. Understood?"

The room was silent for several seconds as the lieutenant looked around, waiting for any questions. It wasn't the type of mission they usually executed, but it was straightforward enough, so no questions were raised.

"Load up!"

Witt

12:00 P.M.

"Approaching target coordinates! Taking heavy fire!" the pilot shouted as Menza was nearly thrown out of his seat by a shield impact.

"No kidding," someone muttered.

"Positions!" the sergeant shouted. The soldiers stood, grabbed hold of overhead cables, then lined up in front of the exits.

"Shields down! You're going to have to jump!" the pilot yelled.

The three sergeants by the doors hit the releases and Menza watched the rear ramp lower to reveal nothing but sky outside.

"Jump!" his sergeant ordered before doing so himself.

The transport took another hit and tilted forward, spilling several of the soldiers towards the cockpit. Menza maintained his position by keeping a firm grip on the cable even as the floor dropped away to leave his feet swinging in the air behind him. Then the craft stabilized, and he ran out the back the moment his feet touched the floor again.

He hit the ground several seconds later and went into a roll to absorb the energy of the impact.

After coming up on his feet he heard an explosion behind him and turned to see his transport spinning out of control with smoke pouring out the back. A few more soldiers managed to jump out, or were flung out, then the craft plowed into the ground.

The private ran to their aid, helping one up and on his way to another when they suddenly came under fire.

He spun around, dove to the ground and returned fire, downing an enemy.

It appeared an entire enemy squad was coming after them, but there was no telling how many of his people managed to make it onto the ground.

He fired a few more times, then realized they were about to be overrun.

Not going to happen.

He laid his rifle on the ground in front of him, pulled out and primed a grenade, then tossed it in front of the approaching enemies and covered his head.

After it exploded he looked up and saw it was clear, so he rose to his feet where he was joined by five of his fellow soldiers. They jogged over to the motionless enemy soldiers where they were surprised to see they were not Amberlins.

"What are Nosines doing here?"

"I've heard stories about this. They're fighting for the confederacy."

"It doesn't matter. We have a job to do," a corporal remarked.

"All units, fall back!" the order came through their headsets.

"Not anymore," Menza observed as several transports and their fighter escorts entered the area. Once the transports landed safely, the fighters broke off and opened fire on the enemy ground positions.

The group made its way to the nearest transport. As they left, a fresh wing of bombers flew in and leveled the complex.

So much for doing things differently.

Ordeos Prime
Saturday, May 1st, 2709
1:03 P.M.

"Majesty, your eldest son is here to see you," the emperor's personal secretary reported via intercom.

"Send him in," Johan ordered without looking up from his work.

He heard the door open and close, but did not look up until the footsteps stopped in front of his desk. When he did, he saw his eleven year old son looking at him with a mixture of apprehension and determination.

"What is it, Son?"

"I think it's time I saw a battle, Father," Kai blurted out.

The emperor leaned back and twirled a stylus in one hand while studying his son.

Tactical training for royal children started at the age of ten, and Kai had eagerly embraced it. One year later, he was well-ahead in his studies. His physical training had been going on for much longer, at which he also excelled.

The schooling schedule which all royals followed didn't have him taking part in a battle for another five years, but perhaps it was time for him to go. After all, Johan always strove to work ahead of any expectations placed on him and it had paid off.

He was proud of his son's initiative, but he needed to make sure he was doing this for the right reasons.

"Why is that?"

"I want to be emperor one day, so I'll need to know what a battle is like if I'm to lead our people."

"You're still young. There is plenty of time to learn all you need to know."

"I want to be the best emperor I can be. The quicker I learn, the *more* I can learn."

"What makes you think you're going to be emperor?"

"I know I will be emperor if I prove my worth to you," Kai responded.

Looking at him, Johan could see the sincerity in his son's eyes. This was not a game to him. He knew full well that if Johan was to choose him as his successor, he had to work for it.

"Very well. Pack your bag and await my instructions."

"I'm packed and ready to go."

"Go to shuttle two. It will take you to the Lentaise Two, which will then take you to the border of the Amberlis Territories. While you are there, you will submit to the authority of Legion Commander Runcis. Is that understood?"

"Yes, Father."

"Then go."

Overjoyed, the prince turned and started running to the door.

"Do not run!"

Obediently slowing down, the prince walked the rest of the way as his father watched him.

That boy was destined to rule the entire human race one day. It was Johan's job to ensure that destiny became reality so all people would know peace and prosperity until the end of time.

9:13 P.M.

The empress stormed into the royal dining area where she found her husband finishing his dinner.

Her political training taking precedence over her anger, she quickly ordered everyone out of the room except for her husband's personal guards.

"What do you think you are doing, sending a twelve year old boy into battle?" she demanded to know.

"It was by his own request, and he will not be involved in any fighting," Johan responded, calmly finishing his wine.

"It doesn't matter if he's involved in the fighting or not! He's a child, and doesn't need to be seeing the horrors of war firsthand!"

"He is potentially the future leader of the greatest empire ever known to mankind, and he recognizes the responsibility that entails. It's time you did as well," Johan stated, rising from his chair and walking to stand in front of her.

"Perhaps his leadership potential is the real reason you sent him out there?"

"What are you implying?"

"Don't forget, I know what you did to your father. Is it possible you now see your son as a threat?"

"What you need to remember is that *I* am the one with Lentaise blood. Any power you hold was granted by me, and I can take it back any time I choose. Do not ever question me," Johan threatened.

"I'm not questioning you," Prailia said in a normal tone of voice, then leaned in and whispered so the personal guard wouldn't hear what she said next.

"I'm telling you. If anything happens to my son, I *will* kill you."

"Guard! Escort the empress to her chambers. Her duties this day have taken a toll on her, and she needs to rest."

"Yes, Majesty," a personal guard responded before walking up beside the empress.

Prailia stared long and hard at her husband, making it abundantly clear she was not afraid of him, then finally turned and left the room.

Chapter Twelve
Cost of Tyranny

Seylin
Friday, May 7th, 2709
11:30 P.M.

"Thank you for agreeing to meet with me, Senators," Leon Tyquese greeted the others as they entered the soft blue glow of his lantern.

He and three senators of the subjugated Seylin Republic were in a muddy field far from the planetary capital, the only place they could meet without being seen by Ordonian soldiers or Star Knights.

A gust of wind ruffled their hair and clothes, blowing the perpetual dust resulting from the Basset bombardments into their covered faces. The Ordonians had installed air purifiers on the planet at the dictatorship's expense, but so far only the cities had seen any noticeable improvement, forcing people to wear goggles and respirators when venturing into undeveloped areas.

Despite all of that, Leon was still glad to be on the ground once again. He might not be able to see much or breathe unassisted, but at least these difficulties were natural. The artificial environment of spaceships just felt so inhuman.

"No, thank you for thinking of us and coming to see us personally. We know that you have considerable responsibilities as president of the confederacy, and are honored you would take the time to speak with us," Senator Powter responded.

"I would add that it is a wonderful and brave thing you are doing in standing against the empire. Your courage brings us hope that we may once again be free," Senator Tuni added.

"Thank you. In fact, it is our struggle against the empire that brings me here. I was hoping you would become the fifth nation to join the Galactic Confederacy and lend your strength to our cause."

"We're not in any position to help you," Senator Kaluan observed.

"The Merchant's Interest was in the same position you are now when they joined us, but they still managed to give us invaluable support in putting the confederacy together. You can do the same when it comes to winning this war."

"How can we do that?"

"Seylin still has considerable mineral wealth, and we have former pirates working with us. If you're willing to share that wealth with us, we can get it off the planet and put it to good use."

"Aren't the Amberlins already providing you with everything you need?"

"The Ordonians have launched an invasion of the territories. We can and will defend them, but an additional source of raw materials would ensure there is no disruption to war production."

"That makes sense."

"In exchange, we can help you form an armed resistance against the Ordonians and eventually the Bassets," Leon offered.

"We are already in the beginning stages of forming a resistance movement, and we need everything we have if we are to put up any real fight, including any minerals we are able to hide from imperial overseers. So the question now becomes, what can you do for us?" Tuni questioned.

This revelation stunned Leon for a moment. Not only had he heard nothing of this before, he was also impressed at their resolve to fight their oppressors.

“A fair question. To start with, we can bring you weapons. We can also loan you the services of a few tacticians if you wish,” he finally offered.

“We're going to need more than that if you want our minerals,” Kaluan demanded.

“I suspect that you have little to no air support for your rebellion. We can provide that as well.”

“How much?”

“As much as you need.”

“How are you going to get all of that onto the planet, or planets when the rebellion spreads?”

“Like I said, we have former pirates working with us. They are very good at what they do,” Leon responded coyly.

“Give us a moment,” Powter requested.

“Of course,” Leon agreed, and the three moved away until all he could see was the glow of their lantern in the dust.

As he waited, Leon compared this meeting to those he'd had with similar officials on Vehla.

Those on Vehla had wanted nothing to do with him or the movement he was building. Not only did they refuse to help in any way, they eventually betrayed him by luring him into a trap and turning him over to the empire.

They no longer cared about individual liberty, only about individual comfort.

Now here he was on another world, meeting with people that weren't even waiting for someone else to come save them. They were willing to fight for their freedom, for what they believed in, no matter the cost.

These strangers understood things his own people seemed to have forgotten.

"We're with you, Mr. President," Powter announced upon the group's return.

"Then may I be the first to welcome the Seylin Republic into the Galactic Confederacy. You have my promise that we won't rest until your freedom is restored."

GCS Justice
Saturday, May 8th, 2709
4:53 A.M.

"Move Squadron Six into position," Sam ordered.

He stared at the map on the tactical room's main screen and reminded himself once again that this was really happening. He was really on the imperial border, leading a powerful fleet intent on penetrating that border and bringing the war home to the Ordonians.

Such a thing hadn't happened for decades.

His enthusiasm for breaching enemy space was tempered by the unfortunate facts of the confederacy's situation. They were not yet powerful enough to break through the border defenses in a full-scale attack, but fighting within imperial space required nothing less than an extensive fleet.

That meant he had to find a way to get dozens of ships through the border without the empire knowing the exact number when they were finished.

Towards that end, he was using jammer vessels to temporarily blind sections of the empire's border sensor grid. Each time they moved through as many ships as they could before imperial patrols could arrive, then moved on to another section chosen at random.

No matter how careful or fast they moved, the Ordonians would still calculate the number of ships crossing their border and intercept before they could gather enough to be a threat. So to supplement his numbers in the time he had to do so, Sam had sent nearly a quarter of his fleet to Asilon IV to send them into imperial space using the alien teleporter. He wanted to send more this way, but Leon overruled him out of fear of raising the empire's suspicion.

He looked at the map of the empire and gave voice to all the feelings he'd carried for the last several years.

"It has been a long time coming, but soon, each and every one of you will know my pain. Your cities will burn. Your friends and family will die. I am coming for you."

New Hope
7:27 A.M.

"Yes. What is it?" Colonel Hikhan Janovich halted his tour of the new Nosine base on the rogue planet when a lieutenant approached him.

"We've finally managed to establish reliable communications with the resistance movement on Eritania thanks to their successful takeover of an Ordonian base."

"Why haven't the Ordonians simply bombed the base into rubble?"

"The base has effective interceptor and anti-air batteries that were undamaged in the takeover."

"Get me a channel to that base immediately," Hikhan ordered, then followed the lieutenant back to the command center.

Normally, communications to and from New Hope were restricted to text messages relayed by satellites every fifteen minutes, but exceptions were made for emergency transmissions. Hikhan was putting this call in that category.

The Nosine base they were in was being constructed in the same canyon as the confederate bases, which were originally the Vehlan and

Pirate bases. It was being built by Nosines and for Nosines, and they had decided to follow the example of the previous bases and build mostly underground within the canyon walls.

This whole thing was President Tyquese's idea. He said that if they were going to be independent they needed their own headquarters.

The suggestion surprised Hikhan in more ways than one. First, he was shocked to see the president following through on his promise to treat the Nosines as equals. Second, he was annoyed that he hadn't thought of this himself. Clearly, he still had a lot to learn about being free.

He entered the command center about halfway up the canyon wall where the lieutenant quickly established a comlink to the planet in question.

"Commander Quinlan of the Eritanian Resistance, sir," he introduced as he stepped aside.

"Colonel Janovich! This is a surprise," Quinlan admitted.

"Good work in taking over that imperial base, commander."

"Thank you, sir. We never could have done it without substantial help from your people."

"As a matter of fact, one of my people is the intent of my call. Do you have a Yanuve Janovich under your command?"

"There is a Yanuve, but I've never had occasion to learn his last name. Janovich?"

"Yes. He is my son."

"One moment. I'll call him up," Quinlan responded before putting the call on hold.

As he waited, Hikhan thought of the last time he saw his son. They were both on Nosin, and Yanuve was boarding a transport to go off-world for the first time. He was being forced to leave, and Hikhan was being forced to stay. The empire was all-powerful, and they had no choice but to obey its commands.

Now they were both soldiers fighting to free their people from their oppressors. How quickly things could change.

The call came back to show Yanuve on the other side, decked out in old, stained, and ill-fitting brown armor.

"Dad?"

"Yanuve!" Hikhan responded, releasing all his pent-up emotions into that one word.

"Well, I never thought I'd be seeing you like this," his son admitted.

"I never thought we could defy the empire and live to tell about it."

"What finally made you change your mind?"

"The timing was right. I'll tell you the whole story sometime, but we can't keep this channel open for very long. What about you? How did you get involved?"

"Not long after we got here, we started hearing rumors about an underground resistance operating on this planet. A few of us were already talking about breaking out and joining them, but then they came and liberated our camp. They told us about the rebellion on Nosin, which our guards had made sure we didn't hear about, and nearly all of us joined them. We've been doing our part ever since," Yanuve explained, the last bit being a jab at Hikhan.

While growing up, Yanuve often expressed his desire to be free, but Hikhan always said it was impossible and that it would only happen if someone else managed to overthrow the empire. His son would respond by saying they had to do their own part if they wanted freedom.

"I'm glad things are working out for all of you. I can't keep this channel open much longer, but I wanted to see that you are safe."

"Wait. What about everyone else?"

"Your mother, brother and sister are all safe. We got them off the planet before the empire reasserted control."

"Ok. Talk to you later then, Dad."

"Bye, Son. Be careful."

Ordeos
8:22 P.M.

The secondary read the new report of an attack on their border sensor grid then filed it away and returned to his work when he saw it was exactly like the others.

Enemy forces kept blinding sensor nodes on their border, but only for one hour or less at a time. This did create a temporary gap in their detection net, but it didn't concern him.

"Should we send a force to investigate, sir?" a captain in the palace's tactical center with him asked.

"There's no need."

"I don't understand, sir. This is the seventh such attack in two days, all on the former Vehlan border. The new sensor net around the former Vehlan territories is still incomplete, so the enemy could move a fleet through there and is now creating these gaps to infiltrate our space."

"That's a possibility, but it's not that simple. First, we do detect them due to the attack on any given node. Second, from the gap that is created and the length of time it takes us to seal it, we can extrapolate how many ships they are moving through. These gaps they are creating are too small for them to bring through enough ships to pose a threat."

"They must still be sending something through, sir. Why ignore them?"

"The only way this tactic makes sense is if they are using it as a distraction to draw our forces away from their real target which is likely something within the Vehlan territories. By keeping our forces where they are, we prevent that attack. Now stop worrying about it and get back to work."

"Understood, sir."

Chapter Thirteen
Trust and Loyalty

Ordeos Prime
Laquenza Spaceport
Sunday, May 16th, 2709
10:30 A.M.

The royal transport settled onto the tarmac and shut off its thrusters as Prailia watched and waited alone, her red dress and dark blonde hair slowly settling back into place after being blown around by the exhaust.

A shuttle normally took royals back and forth from the palace to an orbiting ship, but this time the empress ordered them to bring the prince to the military spaceport. She wanted a chance to talk to him without his father interfering, even going so far as to dismiss her own guards so she could converse with him alone.

The ramp lowered, the door slid open and two Star Knights in full armor stepped out, followed closely by Kai in red and white royal robes and two more knights.

"It is good to see you, Mother," Kai greeted her. While she did not doubt his sincerity, the mother in her still noticed reservation in his tone and features.

Not wanting to discuss things in front of the guards, she gave him a quick hug around the shoulders, then guided him into the back of a waiting limousine after ordering the guards into the middle section so they could be alone.

"Tell me everything," she requested once the motorcade was moving.

"I witnessed a battle in the Amberlis Territories. The space battle I was allowed to watch from a distance. It was strange, appearing more like a fireworks display than a fight," the prince responded, his tone distant.

"What about the ground battle?"

"The legion commander did not allow me to see a live view of that, only a tactical display, but let me walk the battlefield when it was over. It was like nothing I ever imagined," Kai explained, then fell into a brooding silence.

His mother watched him, wishing she could remove the stain that now sat on his soul. While that was something she could not do, she could do her best to ensure it didn't grow into corruption.

"The sight of death and destruction leaves a mark on you that never goes away. It is a heavy burden to bear at your age, and you will never look at war the same way again. Let it make you stronger, but do not allow it to harden your heart," Prailia admonished, to which Kai simply nodded and turned to look out the window.

It was her hope that a spirit of compassion would grow in her son as a result of this experience, that seeing the broken bodies of imperial citizens spread across a battlefield would cause him to feel a greater empathy for his people.

However, she also feared that his heart would harden into one of vengeance. It was possible he would seek retribution against those who killed his people, and that was the beginning of tyranny.

It also occurred to her that instead of developing a greater concern for his people, he would come to see them as disposable. The sight of so many dead might come to feel normal to him, making it easier to sacrifice them for his own purposes.

Their vehicle stopped at the palace entrance and Prailia stepped out first, taking her son's hand when he came out. He did not resist the action.

They walked together to the entrance where they discovered the emperor standing there waiting for them. He ignored his wife and addressed his son to ask how he was doing.

"I am well, Father."

He looked down at the boy and stared at him for several seconds without saying anything.

Then, in a rare show of tenderness, he knelt in front of his son, placed his hands on his shoulders and looked into his eyes.

"You have seen a hard thing, Son, the hardest of all to see. When you think about it, remember that we fight to bring an end to such things. When we reign over all humanity, war will be a thing of the past. People will no longer die in such a horrible fashion, and we will finally be able to reach our true potential as a species."

"I understand," Kai responded. The emperor smiled, patted him on the shoulder, then stood and directed him into the palace while he stayed behind with his wife.

"My sons are not a threat to me. They are my legacy. I will allow no harm to come to them. You should not doubt this," Johan commented to Prailia once their son was out of earshot.

"If you were capable of doing what you did to your father, is it unreasonable for me to think you could the same to your children?"

"My father chose his own fate when he stood in the way of victory and progress. My children are better than he was, and they will rule over the greatest empire ever to grace the stars. It is unreasonable to assume I would do anything to jeopardize that."

"You have shown me you do care. Do not give me any reason to doubt, and I will not do so."

Unknown Place
Unknown Time

The fog swirled thick around the young prince, completely obscuring his vision. He couldn't even see his own feet.

"Is anyone there?" he called out, the fog swirling before him to swallow up his words.

There was no response.

He took a deep breath to steady his nerves, and realized that it wasn't fog. It was smoke, thick and gray but quickly darkening into black.

How had he missed that before?

He covered his mouth and nose with his left hand, then began walking, looking in all directions for any sign of someone else.

Still burning embers soon joined the smoke, along with smells that pierced the smoke and gagged him almost to the point of retching.

As the hand didn't seem to be doing any good, he pulled up his outer robe to cover his lower face and trudged on, feeling more alone than he ever had in his life.

A strong wind arose and finally blew the smoke away but he instantly wished it hadn't.

Now he could see the innumerable corpses covering the ground in all directions and as far as the eye could see. Each one was an Ordonian soldier, and each one was bloodied, burnt, and partially decayed.

Shouts and screams rose in the distance, and they were soon joined by gunfire and explosions.

The prince broke into a run, desperate to escape the horrors surrounding him, but no matter how fast he ran there was no end to the bodies. Thousands, millions, possibly even billions. There was no getting away.

A cliff appeared in front of him and he skidded to a stop at its edge and looked down to see more human remains, but all that was left of these were their bones. He barely recognized the ancient Ordonian uniforms and the weapons still clutched in their skeletal fingers.

"This is our legacy," a voice stated from his right. He turned and saw his ancestor, the first Ordonian emperor Haiden Lentaise, staring at the skeletons.

He looked exactly like he did in all the old paintings and pictures but was wearing anti-ballistic black armor matching the color of his close-cropped hair.

"What do you mean?"

"I started the empire to bring an end to chaos. The human race was on the brink of destroying itself, and our people were the only ones who could save it. Five-hundred years we have dedicated to that goal, and all we have to show for it is death."

"You did what you had to do, as have all the emperors. There wouldn't be so much death if the anarchists stopped resisting the future we're building," the prince encouraged him.

His ancestor finally turned to look him in the eyes, then smiled and laid a hand on his shoulder.

"That is true, but death cannot be our only legacy. Your father will remove all opposition and bring all humanity under our banner. It falls to you to take the next step," he said, then knelt before the prince to punctuate his next point.

"Your forebears have done nothing more than prepare the path. Our way was to destroy, and it was necessary. Your way, and that of your heirs, must be to build. Build the future. Create our *true* legacy."

The prince didn't know what to say, so he said nothing. He'd always expected to continue fighting the anarchists when he became emperor, just like his father. The concept of no war was alien to him.

The first emperor stood up and took a couple steps back, his expression turning stern.

"You must not fail. If you do, the empire will fall, and this is how we will be remembered," he said, then spread his arms wide.

The shouts and screams that had remained in the distance this entire time now grew louder, and kept growing like rising floodwaters until they threatened to drown both of them.

It became too much and he clamped his hands over his ears as he fell to his knees in agony.

"Make it stop!" he cried out.

"Prince Kai! Wake up!"

He shot up into a sitting position, nearly colliding with the Star Knight who'd been shaking him, but the knight's reflexes proved true and he jumped out of the way in time.

"Wha?" he managed to get out.

"You were having a nightmare, Highness. Are you alright?"

His heart still racing, Prince Kai looked around the room, the familiar settings calming him. He didn't respond until he was firmly back in reality.

"Yes, I'm fine."

"Are you sure? I can send for your parents if you need."

"No, that isn't necessary. Return to your post," the prince ordered. The knight hesitated, but eventually bowed and did as he was told.

He laid back down and stared at the ceiling as he reflected on his dream.

Build the future. Create our true legacy.

What was that supposed to mean?

OES Lentaise Four
Monday, March 29th, 2709
6:00 A.M.

Upon entering the officer's gym Canza spotted Ricine on the far side facing the mirror while doing leg squats, her well-toned legs and arms clearly visible thanks to her shorts and sleeveless top. Sweat had darkened her blonde hair and plastered it to the sides of her face, but her breathing remained steady as she finished her set and switched to overhead extensions.

This was the first time Canza had ever seen her out of uniform, so he decided it was the perfect time to learn more about her and made his way over.

"Morning, Knight," he greeted as he started his stretches.

"Morning, Primary," she responded, showing only a hint of exertion.

He finished his stretches, then picked up a couple weights of his own and began doing bicep curls, using the time to choose his next words carefully.

"What are your thoughts on the progress of the war?" he finally asked.

"It's going slower than it should."

"You fear we'll be defeated?"

"No, but the confederacy was allowed to grow into a real threat which undermines our ability to secure a quick victory."

"So you trust in the empire's strength?" Canza pressed, choosing to ignore the insinuation of his earlier failure.

She shot him a suspicious look, clearly wondering where he was going with this line of questioning.

"Yes," she eventually answered.

"What about the emperor? Do you trust his strength?"

"Yes."

She finished her set, replaced her weights on the rack, then grabbed a heavier one and began doing squats.

He didn't speak while she did this under the guise of thinking over her answers and completed several more repetitions before continuing.

"What about his leadership? Do you trust that?"

Ricine dropped the dumbbell on the floor and turned to look at him, waiting for him to stop exercising and look her in the eyes before responding.

"What is the purpose of this, Canza?"

"We've been working together for some time now, and will continue doing so for the foreseeable future. If we're to continue going into battle together, I feel it's important I know where you stand," he explained.

"Is that so?" she questioned, clearly not convinced.

"Are you avoiding my question for a reason?" Canza challenged. Her bright green eyes narrowed angrily at the implied accusation, but she maintained her composure.

"I trust the emperor's leadership implicitly."

"So your loyalty is without question?"

"I am a Star Knight, sworn to serve and defend the royal family until my dying breath. My loyalty has been tested and approved by people far more qualified to do so than you."

"What if I were to tell you the emperor ordered troops on Vehla to open fire on civilians without cause. Would you remain loyal?"

"If the emperor gave such an order, there had to be a cause."

"True. Perhaps such a cause can be found in the confederacy's successful invasion of the Magnin Kingdom, the conquest of which was carried out by the emperor himself. I wonder if the fact a Vehlan led that invasion would prompt him to do such a thing."

"You're lying. The emperor never gave such an order. I know for a fact nothing like that has happened."

"What if it never happened only because Vehla's governor stepped in and stopped it?"

"If that were true, the governor would have been arrested for treason. Since we are not talking through prison bars right now, that obviously didn't happen either."

"What I'm hearing from you is that if this were true, it would cause you to question your loyalty," Canza challenged.

The knight leaned forward within inches of Canza's face and whispered, "My loyalty is without question."

When he didn't say anything else, she put her dumbbell back in the rack then stormed off.

6:29 A.M.

Her small quarters only allowed Wendy Ricine five steps before she was forced to turn and resume her pacing in the other direction which served only to add to her mounting frustration.

She needed to shower and don her uniform, but nothing else mattered until she figured out what had just happened.

Why would Primary Canza question her loyalty?

What right did he have to treat one of the emperor's knights in such a way?

How did such thoughts ever occur to him?

She suddenly stopped at the foot of her bed when a new possibility entered her mind.

He wasn't asking questions because he doubted her loyalty, but rather because it was his loyalty that was wavering and he wanted to know if she would agree with his doubts.

The more she thought about it, the more that conclusion made sense, which meant she should report the conversation to Master Knight Penavel, but if she did Canza would be arrested and possibly executed.

Why should that be a problem for her?

That question set her to pacing again, which reminded her of how worked up she had been when it had seemed he was questioning her integrity.

Why would his opinion matter that much to her?

She shook her head to clear it of those nuisances and returned to the question of why Max Canza might be doubting his commitment to the empire.

The two of them had worked together for over a year now, and she was studying him closely the entire time. As she reviewed his actions over that time she realized there could be no doubt about his loyalty. Everything he did was for the good of the empire and rarely for his own benefit.

Then she realized that his questions were themed more about loyalty to the emperor specifically, not the empire as a whole. Most thought they were one and the same, but could it be Canza thought differently? It was no secret that Secondary Zenzal did.

If that was the case, then it was his loyalty to Emperor Johan Lentaise that was wavering, not his loyalty to the empire. From what she'd learned of him, that would only happen if he came to believe Lentaise was a threat to the empire.

Was that scenario he posed about killing civilians on Vehla purely hypothetical or did something like that actually happen?

She sat down at the room's computer, interfaced her palco to use the codes stored within, then searched through recent transcripts from the Vehlan planetary government and garrison.

It didn't take long for her to find an order direct from the emperor to the legion commander telling him to begin randomly firing on civilians. The follow-up report showed that the only reason he didn't do this was because he contacted Canza for confirmation first who then told him to wait. Lentaise rescinded the order shortly after that.

So he was telling the truth. If this order had been obeyed, it probably would have led to the people rebelling, and not only on Vehla.

She deactivated the computer and leaned back to stare at the blank screen.

The information made little difference in the end. It was still her duty to report suspected disloyalty on the part of any citizen, but there was no solid evidence Primary Canza intended any harm.

There was no doubt if she reported the encounter nothing would stop the master knight from using it to discredit and destroy him.

That shouldn't matter to her, but there was no denying it did.

It was her duty to monitor the loyalty of imperial citizens and stop threats to the emperor, but there was no threat here and Canza was clearly committed to the empire and its future, so there was nothing she needed to do.

Her decision made, she finally went to take a shower and wash off the sweat which had now dried into a thick film coating her skin.

Canza saved her life once, now she'd saved his.

Ordeos

10:00 A.M.

From his position on the throne, Johan watched with an amused smile as the praetor of Swint and his entourage walked the distance to the throne and bowed before him.

Normally he left politics like this to his empress, but this particular meeting aroused his curiosity. They'd recently sent a fleet through Swint's territory to reach the Amberlis Territories, so he suspected the praetor was here to complain.

An amusing concept.

"Emperor and Empress Lentaise, thank you for agreeing to meet me," Praetor Denlock greeted upon concluding his bow.

"What is it you want that couldn't have been handled by our respective ambassadors?" Johan asked bluntly.

"My nation wishes to join the empire," Denlock replied, surprising the emperor. He looked at Prailia from the corner of his eye whom he could tell was equally as surprised but hiding it well.

"Is that so? Why would that be?" he questioned, focusing back on his guest.

"It is only a matter of time before each nation must choose a side in this war of yours. Your recent bombing of Ascion as well as the intrusion on my own territory indicate the war will spread even to those who have not chosen a side. It's also no secret the Galactic Confederacy is working to bring more nations under its banner. We have chosen to enter this war on our terms before being forced to do so."

"Why not side with the confederacy?"

"After ending the war with the Vehlan Union, the empire demonstrated a desire for peace in how it treated the Vehlans. All the confederacy has achieved is to plunge even more nations into another war. My people want peace, not war."

"Commendable. You have sight where most others are blind," Prailia commented.

"You do understand that joining the empire means full assimilation? You will no longer be your own nation, but rather provinces of the greater Ordeon Empire," Johan interjected.

"That's not the deal you made with the Basset Dictatorship."

"That was a unique circumstance which we chose to exploit for our own ends. You have come to us and I am telling you what will happen if you go through with this."

"We understand and this possibility was put before our senate, but the measure still passed nearly unanimously."

"Nobody decides to do such a thing merely for the sake of peace. What exactly are you hoping to get out of this?"

"We become a part of the empire in exchange for all those currently in power receiving similar positions within the new order."

"What do you have to offer to warrant such a concession on our part?"

"We've noticed your fleet focuses heavily on bigger, stronger ships, allowing you to bring significant firepower to a fight. However, this leaves your military lacking in the area of speed, granting your enemies a means of escape," the praetor started to explain.

"This is inconsequential. Our enemies are always run to ground eventually," Johan interrupted.

"True, but we propose never letting them get away in the first place. We recently created an Interceptor Class Frigate, six of which are already in operation. If I may?" Denlock told them, then held up his left hand to indicate he wanted to transfer a file using his palco.

Johan signaled Penavel, who accepted the file first and inspected it for malware before passing it on to the emperor and empress.

When he brought it up, Johan saw it was design specifications for the ship.

"Give me a summary," he demanded.

"This ship is the fastest ever built, but still carries a fair amount of firepower. Three of them working together could even take down a destroyer."

"I doubt that. According to this, combat shielding is minimal."

"Shields are only necessary if you get hit. With the right pilot, this ship can easily outmaneuver the shots from a larger ship. All of this makes it perfect as an escort for larger vessels, search and destroy missions, and border patrol duties. Thanks to its speed, one ship can patrol twice the territory of any other vessel," Denlock explained.

"And you think this is enough to buy you inclusion into the empire, as well as positions of power for your people?" Johan questioned after deactivating his palco.

"Yes, I do," Denlock responded confidently, but Johan spotted a flash of fear in his eyes.

Perfect.

"We are already designing a ship class similar to this. The Vehlans are well-known for their space races, and many of them are happily providing us with their knowledge. What makes your ship of any value to me?" he questioned.

The whole thing was a lie but he wanted to make this man work for what he wanted.

"Ours is already in production."

"True, but we could always take it from you. You wouldn't be able to stop us, and we could still make your nation part of the empire without having to give you and the other government officials anything."

"Such an action takes time, and resources. Why waste those things when we are giving you everything we have freely?"

The emperor leaned back into his seat and pretended to think the matter over while staring his guest in the eyes.

Denlock broke out into a sweat and his eyes darted from the emperor to the empress and back again as Johan dragged it out for several minutes.

"I accept your offer. Prailia, Penavel, see to it the nation of Swint is absorbed into the empire," he finally ordered.

He rose with a flourish, descended the dais steps and left the room without giving anyone another look.

Chapter Fourteen
Borders

New Hope
Wednesday, June 1st, 2710
3:23 A.M.

"It's been over a year now and we have nothing to show for this war but death and destruction!" Leon vented.

He required himself to always maintain at least the appearance of total confidence in front of others, but alone he could express himself as needed.

Unable to sleep, he'd been staring at the galactic map on the wall to the right of his desk for over an hour, trying to find some hope their struggle would end soon.

That hope did not come. All he found was despair.

Since starting the war against the Ordeon Empire, the confederacy had managed to liberate the Merchant's Interest, but not fully. Even now, Ordonian ground forces still held several positions and ongoing fighting had all but wrecked the economy. The significant financial boost which was part of his plan for ending this war quickly was not going to come.

They had also lent military support to the Magnins and helped liberate their kingdom but failed to bring them into the confederacy. Despite the fact they were both fighting the same enemy, their relationship continued to be strained at best.

The Ordonians had retaliated by attacking the planet Ascion which was considering joining the confederacy at the time but now was nothing but a ball of ash.

With the help of Sam and his pirates, or troopers as they were now called, the Nosines rebelled and freed their homeworld for a short time, but that was now firmly under imperial control once again. The rebellion continued to rage elsewhere and Nosine divisions were fighting as part of the confederacy's military, but little ground had been won in gaining their freedom.

A more recent achievement was to help the Seylins free their home system from the empire's clutches, but they were still unable to join the larger war. All their resources were currently tied up in preventing the imperial equipped Basset Dictatorship from regaining control.

After successfully infiltrating imperial territory, Sam managed to capture the systems of Raxin and Erebus, but was now stuck there. He was capable of fending off Ordonian attempts to drive him out, but could not attack another system without spreading himself too thin.

Meanwhile, the empire had secured some victories of its own.

Two nations, Swint and Jinara, had chosen to become part of the empire in response to what they were calling the confederacy's threat to "galactic peace and stability." They remained silent while the Imps attacked nations left and right, but then got upset when someone took a stand.

Nearly the entire Vaton Conglomerate was now occupied territory. All that remained was their homeworld which was protected by powerful ground to space weaponry forcing the empire to set up a blockade instead of invading.

This was due in part to its government deciding to send away most of its military to join the confederate campaigns and only offer marginal resistance to the invasion knowing their homeworld was well-protected. It was not something Leon would have asked of them, but the pragmatic

Vatons understood that winning the larger war was more important than hanging on to their own territory.

So much death and destruction, with nothing more than a stalemate to show for it.

He'd given up asking himself the question of whether or not it was worth it. The empire had to be stopped. There was no question about that.

The question that now occupied his thoughts was if the effort was wasted. If they failed to win this war, all the sacrifice would be for nothing.

He glanced at the confederate flag which now adorned the wall behind his desk with the galaxy logo in its center surrounded by the words 'Stronger Together'. There were a lot of people counting on him to put that strength to good use and find a way through this. He couldn't let them down.

Ordeos Prime
9:30 A.M.

"Reporting as ordered, Majesties," Primary Canza said as he bowed before the thrones.

"Your successful invasion of the Vaton Conglomerate has restored my faith in you, Primary. Do not make the mistake of losing it again," Emperor Johan Lentaise commented.

"Your success on Vehla is also to be commended. Royal inspectors report the planet is ready to become a fully recognized province of the empire," Empress Prailia Lentaise added.

"You do me great honor, Majesties. I do believe that we have managed to stabilize all fronts in the war, and the people of Vehla have come a long way. They wish only for peace and prosperity and see us as the ones that can bring it."

"Good. What is your perspective on the war at large?" Johan questioned impatiently.

"The efforts of both sides have stalled. Each side is currently operating in a primarily defensive mode and using only small fleets on the offensive. These fleets are unable to take and hold territory and only serve to test the other's defenses and conduct occasional raids."

"What do you plan to do about this?"

"Nothing."

"Excuse me?"

"We tighten our defenses, secure our recent conquests, and build our forces. An offensive action at this time would harm our cause."

"More so than the enemy fleet still in our territory?"

"They do not have the capacity to attack anywhere else and Raxin and Erebus are not strategically necessary for victory. My recommendation is to keep sending small attacks to wear them down, but driving them out would require too much right now," Canza insisted.

"I want a plan presented to me within the next twenty-four hours for the destruction of that fleet, then I'll decide if it is practical," the emperor commanded.

"Yes, Majesty," Canza agreed, at which point Johan glanced at Master Knight Penavel, signaling him to take over.

"There is also the matter of the new armor being made available to the Star Knights," Penavel revealed.

"Oh, that. You'll be happy to know I'm satisfied with its performance, and Ricine seems to be as well. All we need is for the knights to provide us with specifics on any modifications they need done."

"Why hasn't Knight Ricine reported this?"

"I haven't told her the armor is ready."

"Why not?"

"I've been busy," Canza replied nonchalantly, eliciting an angry glare from the master knight.

Before anyone could respond, Secondary Zenzal rushed into the room and whispered something to the primary.

"What's going on?" Johan questioned.

"The common border is under attack by a rogue nation. The defenders are claiming they cannot hold and are requesting reinforcements," Canza answered.

The common border surrounded all of the legitimately recognized nations, or the Core Nations. A stipulation of the treaty that formed it was each nation that signed on had to contribute to its defense against the hundreds of pirate factions beyond it, the likes of which made the pirates inside the border seem civilized. There were also rogue nations that were deemed hazardous to overall peace and stability.

"Do we have any ships in the area?" Johan asked.

"One destroyer. The rest were recalled to fight in the wars," Canza responded, referring to both the Hundred Years War and the current conflict.

"Send it to the area. That will be enough to honor the treaty and we have more important matters which require our attention."

"I respectfully disagree, Your Majesty. I believe we should dispatch a squadron to the area immediately."

"It will take weeks to get there, and who knows how long to get back!" Penavel argued.

"You just said we don't have the resources to launch an offensive against the confederacy so why waste what we do have on something so far away?" Johan asked.

"There is no doubt the confederacy will send aid in the hopes of gaining favor with more nations. We could exploit that action in the short-term to gain some ground, but I feel it is more important to prevent more nations from joining our enemies," Canza explained.

"You doubt our ability to defeat these potential newcomers?"

"No, Majesty. It is only a matter of time before we defeat all who oppose us. My only concern is how much time. The more we have to fight at once, the longer it will take," Canza responded.

The emperor leaned back to think the matter over while watching the primary with a wry grin, causing him to feel as though he were somehow being tested.

"Send the squadron," he finally ordered, and Canza nodded at Zenzal who rushed off to get it done.

"If there's nothing further, Majesties, I need to return to my duties," Canza commented.

"What about the armor?" Penavel interjected.

"I wasn't talking to you, unless I missed the announcement where you became emperor," Canza shot back, feeling a surge of victory when both the emperor and empress gave Penavel annoyed looks.

"You may return to your duties. Ricine will get with you soon about the armor," Johan ordered.

"As you wish, Highness."

GCS Justice
9:43 A.M.

The general stared at the red and black surface of the planet Erebus displayed on the bridge's main screen and wondered if it and the nearly abandoned surface of Raxin would be the only Ordonian planets he would ever see.

"Incoming transmission from New Hope, General."

"Put it through," Sam ordered, bracing himself for whatever came next. If Leon was sending a live transmission, it had to be bad.

"We've received a distress call from the common border. It's about to be breached," Leon reported the moment the connection was made.

“I feel for them, but we have other concerns at the moment.”

“We have an obligation to help in the defense.”

“No, we don't. The confederacy hasn't signed on to the Core Treaty.”

“It doesn't matter. If the border is breached, we're all in danger.”

“I disagree. It would take decades or centuries for any of those rogues to get far enough through the outer nations to threaten us, if ever. We need our people here, fighting the Imps.”

“The confederacy is about helping people, Sam. We can't continue claiming that if we leave other nations to burn because their problems are not our own,” Leon insisted. He was right, of course, but Sam wasn't about to admit that.

“Even if we were to send an expedition, it will take weeks for them to get there. The fighting will be over long before that.”

“Use the technology on Asilon Four to shave two days off the journey. The nations behind the border should hold long enough for our reinforcements to arrive.”

“Alright, I'll send the ships. Let's just hope the empire doesn't kick us in the teeth while they're gone,” Sam finally agreed.

GCS Maluesi
Saturday, June 11th, 2710
1:02 P.M.

“About time we got here. Drop us out of hyperspace,” Captain Jansen ordered.

This was his first mission since his promotion and it was to clean up a mess in the backside of the galaxy. All he wanted to do was finish this and get back.

At least his ship was a Vehlan destroyer which should help make it happen faster.

"Firefight in progress, sir," Tactical reported once they were in normal space.

"Condition red! Let me see it!" Jansen ordered.

An alarm sounded and a tactical display appeared on the bridge's main screen to show ships of the Brazark Federation engaged in combat against vessels of unknown allegiance.

"We're being hailed by the federation."

"Put it through," the captain ordered, and half the main screen changed to the image of a colonel. From the transmission, one could see the ship he was on had taken considerable damage and the colonel was bleeding from a cut on the cheek.

"Identify yourself," he demanded.

"Captain Tom Jansen of the Galactic Confederacy. We are here to render assistance."

"Then what are you waiting for?" the colonel responded then severed the connection.

"You're welcome," Jansen muttered to himself before addressing his crew. "All ships, attack."

"What formation, sir?"

"It doesn't matter. These guys don't stand a chance against us. Just wipe them out."

"Yes, sir."

Upon seeing the confederate ships speeding towards the battle, several of the rogue vessels turned away from the Brazarks and formed up to intercept them. Some of the others fled to hyperspace while the rest continued attacking their original targets.

The confederates opened fire and destroyed or disabled most of their attackers in the first volley. Three ships were left, but two surrendered and the third escaped into hyperspace.

When they saw what happened, all those still fighting the Brazarks also chose to surrender or run.

"See, no need for formations," Jansen commented.

“Brazark colonel hailing again,” Communications reported, and Jansen signaled him to put it through with a wave of his hand.

“Thank you for your help, Captain. This is the biggest attack the rogues have ever made, and they might have gotten us if you hadn't shown up.”

“Why launch such an attack now?” Jansen questioned.

“The news of your war with the Ordeon Empire, and how far it's spread, has reached us even this far out. They probably learned of it as well and figured ships were pulled out of the border to fight,” the colonel explained.

“Speaking of, we need to get back to that war. Can you finish up here?”

“This was the last of what they had. We'll be fine.”

“Glad to hear it,” Jansen told the colonel then addressed his crew, “Set course for Rally Point Alpha, full speed.”

Vehla
Monday, June 13th, 2710
1:47 P.M.

“What is it?” Canza questioned once the comlink with Zenzal was established in his governor's office.

“Our squadron has arrived at the Common Border. They report that the confederacy beat us to it and already repelled the invasion. What are your orders?”

“Was it pirates attacking, or one of the rogue nations?”

“A nation.”

“Send them in to wipe it out. Destroy everything then return.”

“Yes, sir.”

Chapter Fifteen
Echoes

New Hope
Tuesday, June 14th, 2710
10:51 A.M.

"Our base is complete and our newest recruits are trained. We are ready to get back in the fight," Colonel Janovich reported to President Tyquese after taking a seat in his office.

"Where are you going?" Leon asked.

"Sir?"

"Call it another step in the journey towards freedom. You can't have someone making the decisions for you all the time. You know the Nosine rebellion better than I do. Where are your new reinforcements most needed?" Tyquese explained.

Surprised by the president's question, the colonel was unable to respond right away. While he thought, Tyquese leaned back in his chair and patiently waited for him to speak.

"I believe we would be of the most use within the Vehlan territories, specifically the system of Redlode," Janovich finally suggested.

"Why there?"

"Our rebellion has spread to most of our people the empire brought in to rebuild the Vehlan territories, but those on Redlode haven't even heard about it. The moment fighting first broke out on Nosin the empire enacted a strict no-travel policy for slaves regarding Redlode.

No one coming in, no one going out. We can recruit those already on the planet to the cause, and disrupt Ordonian fuel shipments in the process. From what I've heard, it was the loss of this planet that caused the union's defeat in The Hundred Years War. Perhaps we can do the same in reverse," Janovich explained.

"Perhaps you can. I agree with your assessment. Take a division to the planet and do precisely as you suggest."

"Only one division?"

"That should be more than enough to start a rebellion. General Tyquese needs the rest on his campaign."

"Understood," Janovich responded. The president was about to say something else, but a notification ding on his computer drew his attention.

"Something wrong?" Janovich questioned.

"No, it's just a report from Captain Jansen. I wasn't expecting it until he got back," Tyquese replied, then opened the message. As he read it, his demeanor morphed from quiet confidence to profound confusion.

Noticing the change, the colonel asked what was going on.

"The nation we assisted at the Common Border just finished interrogating the prisoners they took and thought we should know what they learned. Apparently, the reason these rogues were so intent on getting through the border is because they felt something was attacking them. Something coming from uninhabitable regions of space."

OES Lentaise Four
11:04 A.M.

"Something was attacking them? That isn't unusual on the other side of the border," Primary Canza observed.

"Apparently, these were no mere pirates, or even another rogue nation. According to the prisoners our people captured, a couple weeks ago all the outposts on their border nearest the galactic core went dark. They sent a couple ships to investigate, but they went missing. Finally, they sent an entire squadron, but it also disappeared without a trace. When the first civilian system also went dark, they panicked and attacked the border en masse," Secondary Zenzal explained.

"Sounds like they let their imaginations get the best of them. Our ships went through the entire territory, correct?"

"Yes, sir."

"Did they find anything suspicious?"

"They did report that upon arriving at the system in question they found that all the life on every planet and moon in the system was dead. People, animals, plants. Everything. Their scans detected massive amounts of neutron radiation but that is all."

"That explains it. A radiation storm swept through the system, killing everyone before they could evacuate or even call for help."

"What about the border outposts?"

"There's no telling what could have happened that close to the galactic core. Either way, the border is secure once again and whatever prompted the rogues to attack is no threat to us. We have bigger issues to deal with."

"So what's our next target?"

"Atrias. We've learned that this is where the confederacy is building its dreadnaughts and carriers. We will deprive them of those shipyards, then this war will end."

Chapter Sixteen
No More Stalemate

AS Defender
Friday, June 17th, 2710
9:07 A.M.

"I've gone from leading my own pirate faction to being Tyquese's lackey," Captain Nick Jaeger, formally known as the pirate captain Brown Nick, complained.

He was given command of an Atrian destroyer shortly after the war broke out and assigned as a liaison between the confederate forces guarding that nation and its own defense teams, but the whole thing was only a means to keep him out of the way. Atrias only comprised a single star system and was days from the Ordonian border so why would they ever bother to attack it?

"We could always go independent again. The others would surely follow your lead and this ship would give us a significant advantage," Commander Penski, Jaeger's second-in-command, suggested.

"Tyquese would hunt us down and kill us."

"We can go to one of the nations closer to the Common Border. Red Sam has bigger problems than us," Penski argued.

It was an intriguing proposition, but it meant leaving behind everything they had.

"Hyperspace window detected! It's the Ordonians!" Tactical suddenly called out.

"Condition Red! Turn to face them!" Jaeger ordered, but the enemy had already opened fire and their ship took several direct hits before the combat shields could be raised.

"All ships, return fire!"

"They outnumber us, two to one!"

"I said, RETURN FIRE!"

The confederates shot back, but it did little to slow their enemy who seemed to shrug off the lasers and missiles as they sped towards the border patrol.

Two Ordonian destroyers headed straight for the Defender, weapons blazing.

The ship shook violently under the assault and the crew struggled to remain at their stations even with the seat restraints.

Sparks flew from consoles, lights blew out, and someone screamed in pain, but the captain refused to give up.

"Full-speed ahead! Turn thirty degrees! Put starboard enemy vessel between us and the other one!" he barked out orders.

"We should retreat!" Penski called out.

"No! Tyquese thinks me incapable! I'm going to prove him wrong!"

"At least call for reinforcements!"

"All border positions under heavy attack, Captain!" Tactical reported, making reinforcements unlikely.

"We can do this!"

The Defender came up alongside its target and fired everything it had at the same time as the Ordonians, but the other ship proved to be far superior.

Lights exploded and showered the bridge with sparks and glass.

Consoles blew up in their operators' faces and pelted them with shrapnel.

Fires erupted and filled the bridge with smoke.

People screamed.

Powerful explosions rocked the ship, one of which sent the captain flying from his chair with a loud ripping sound as the fiber connections between uniform and seat tore out.

He flew towards the space between Helm's and Navigation's chairs but managed to put out his arms in time to avoid hitting his head on the underside of their console.

Silence fell save for the crackling of fires and the whoosh of suppression systems.

The captain extricated himself from under the console and staggered to his feet then coughed violently as his eyes teared up from the smoke.

His right sleeve hung loose on his arm from where it was ripped, so he tore it off the rest of the way and placed it over his mouth so he could breathe, then checked himself for blood but didn't find anything.

When the smoke finally cleared enough for him to see the bridge he saw that nearly everyone was on the floor. Most weren't moving and those that were did so slowly, groaning with the effort.

One of the unmoving figures lay next to the captain's chair and he walked up to it then turned it over to see that it was Penski, his eyes open wide and frozen in a look of sheer terror.

The captain collapsed into his chair and rubbed his forehead. He'd never particularly liked Penski but he had been good at his job and would be difficult to replace.

"Status report?" he eventually asked of anyone still capable of answering.

"Severe damage, sir. We're operating on emergency life support only."

"Do we have any idea how the battle is going?"

"I saw reinforcements come in before my display went out, but there's no way to tell now."

"They're probably still fighting then," Jaeger commented, then fell silent.

The only people that moved were those tending the fires and the wounded while the captain just sat there with his head in his hand until someone finally spoke up.

"What do we do, sir?"

"I don't know."

GCS Firestarter
11:33 A.M.

"Drop us right in the middle of them," Captain David Saxen ordered.

His assault group was restocking at an Amberlin outpost when he'd received word of an attack against Atrias causing him to immediately set course with every available ship.

"Aye, sir," Helm responded.

An instant later they were in normal space where they were greeted by two bright flashes of light.

The tactical display showed that two of the enemy ships, a cruiser and destroyer, had exploded upon their exit but it also showed that two of Saxen's ships were simply gone.

That could only mean those vessels had collided during re-entry, which went to show the danger of coming out so close to ships already in normal space.

"Fire at will!" Saxen ordered.

Each of his remaining seven ships chose its own target and opened fire, forcing the imperial ships to spread apart in an attempt to get away.

"Stay with them!"

The troopers stayed with their targets, allowing them no breathing room. The Ordonians fought back with little effect, their disrupted coordination preventing them from causing much damage.

Emboldened by the sight of fresh reinforcements, the Atrian defenders charged in and followed the example of the troopers by getting in close to the enemy ships and firing everything they had.

Three more imperial ships were eliminated while only one confederate was lost.

The Ordonians finally gave up trying to regroup and fled into hyperspace, narrowly missing their assailants in the process.

The Firestarter's bridge crew let out a victorious cheer, all except for David. He knew it wasn't going to be that easy and they needed to prepare for another wave as soon as possible.

"Where is Brown Nick anyway? Isn't he supposed to be overseeing these defenses?" the captain asked of no one in particular.

"I just checked. His ship was disabled early in the battle and the Atrians have been too busy to send rescue craft," Commander Winters answered.

"Of course. Leave it to that idiot to nearly let the Ordonians through."

"I thought Browns were supposed to be good at defense?"

"I've always thought that was a misinterpretation. They're hoarders. For some reason, people seem to think that means they're good at protecting what they're hoarding. More likely nobody wants the junk, so nobody ever tries to steal it," David explained.

"I see."

"Get me the commander of the Atrian defense. I'll take care of this myself."

3:22 P.M.

"Keep fighting!" Saxen demanded.

"There are too many of them, sir! We have to retreat!" Winters shouted after the ship took another hard hit.

"No! All ships move in on my target!" Saxen ordered as he marked the target on his command console.

Only five confederate ships remained battle-worthy, but each one obeyed and charged the moderately damaged Ordonian destroyer along with a couple dozen fighters.

Out of fear of hitting their own ship, the other enemy ships reduced their attacks in favor of moving into positions for cleaner shots. The besieged destroyer continued firing but it was hard for capital ship weapons to hit small, moving targets at such close ranges.

The troopers took advantage of this weakness and pummeled the destroyer until it was disabled a couple minutes later.

Unfortunately, this left them surrounded by the rest of the enemy fleet. A single volley at this point would destroy them.

"They're calling for our surrender," Tactical reported, the exhaustion plain in his voice.

Captain Saxen stared at the main screen showing the dozen enemy ships surrounding them, but he didn't respond.

"There is nothing to be gained by our deaths," Winters suggested.

"We're dead either way. The confederacy may have granted us amnesty, but I doubt the empire will be as generous. Inform the Atrians it is their choice on whether or not to surrender. I know the rest of us would prefer to go down fighting," Saxen responded.

"Yes, sir," Winters acquiesced, then nodded at Tactical to send the transmission.

Before he could do so, several ships dropped out of hyperspace and took up positions around the imperial fleet.

"They're ours! Three dreadnaughts and carriers along with all their support vessels! They're calling for the Imps' surrender!" Tactical exclaimed.

Before anyone could say anything else, most of the Ordonian ships turned and opened fire on the confederate reinforcements while the rest opened up on Saxen and his ships.

"Full speed ahead! Fire at will!" Saxen ordered.

"Incoming transmission from the lead dreadnaught, sir," Tactical reported and Saxen nodded as a signal to put it through.

"Sorry we're late, Captain, but these ships weren't set to be launched for another two weeks. It took us a while to get them ready for battle," the dreadnaught commander said via audio only.

"We're glad you were able to make it all. Let's get this done," Saxen responded, then cut the connection.

Infused with new energy, Saxen's remaining ships charged the enemy. One of the other gunships was destroyed on the way, but the rest made it.

The dreadnaughts and carriers were keeping the enemy capitol ships busy, so they went to work on the enemy fighters.

4:19 P.M.

"Well, it's about time," David commented when the last enemy ship was finally destroyed.

"Sir, we're receiving a distress call from Captain Jaeger. He and his crew are in lifepods requesting pickup," Tactical reported, ruining the moment for the captain.

"His ship's carcass must have finally run out of air."

"Should we go get him, sir?"

"I'm tempted to just let him rot."

"Personally, I think what General Tyquese will do to him will be far more satisfying," Winters suggested.

David smiled at the thought and gave the order to pick up all the lifepods.

The general could be pretty nasty when he wanted to be.

GCS Justice
Saturday, June 18th, 2710
10:33 A.M.

"You were assigned to protect Atrias, which seemed to be an ideal assignment for the leader of the brown faction, yet you failed. Miserably," General Sam Tyquese summarized.

Holograms of Captains Jaeger and Saxen stood before him in the center of the conference table, one answering for a failure which the other had to fix.

"There were too many! I tried to fight them, but...," Jaeger started to say.

"You *tried* to fight them!" Tyquese roared, causing the captain to shrink away from him in fear despite the fact he couldn't actually do anything to him. A satisfied smirk spread across Saxen's face as he glanced at his colleague.

"I used everything I had. There wasn't anything I could do."

"You claim there wasn't anything you could do, yet Captain Saxen managed to successfully defend against not just *one*, but *two* attacks. How do you explain that?"

"He received reinforcements."

"Irrelevant. He managed to hold the enemy long enough for those reinforcements to arrive, which is what you should have done. Why didn't you?"

"I tried."

This time the general's only reply was to rub his forehead in frustration.

The man obviously wasn't command material, regardless of the mission. Why had it taken him so long to see it?

"Your incompetence amazes me, Jaeger. How you ever got to be a pirate captain is beyond me," he finally said while keeping his hand over his face.

"Incompetent! I've stolen far more than you ever did," Jaeger responded, his anger temporarily overtaking his fear and the general lowered his hand to look his subordinate in the eye.

"Your actions have proven to me that you are unfit for military service, which normally leads to a dishonorable discharge. However, I think that would be going too easy on you. You are hereby stripped of all rank and condemned to serve the remainder of this war in an Amberlin mine, which also serves as a maximum security prison. Resist in any way and you will be summarily executed."

The condemned man stepped forward as if to argue his punishment, but was stopped when Saxen placed a hand on his shoulder.

"As for what you own as a pirate captain, that is now forfeit. Fifty percent will be evenly split between Captain's Saxen and Turley as reward for their exemplary service while I will hold the rest to give to your replacement," Tyquese dealt out the last of the punishment.

This time, Jaeger made the wise choice to stay silent and was soon dragged off by Saxen before the connection was cut.

With that out of the way, the general made his way back to the bridge. He had a war to fight.

New Hope
Saturday, April 23rd, 2710
8:33 P.M.

"Send her in," Leon told his assistant.

"I wasn't actually expecting you to be here this late," the Vaton scientist commented as she walked up to his desk. She was one of several scientists stationed on New Hope to study the oddity of a life-sustaining rogue planet while also researching methods of maintaining a larger population and the president occasionally gave them other tasks related to the war.

"What else would I be doing?" he questioned as he waved towards a chair, and she sat on the forward edge.

"Most people are relaxing at this hour, either in their quarters or out with a few friends."

"I don't have any time for that. I never have. There is too much work to be done."

"You have to relax sometime."

"I will relax when tyranny is vanquished. What is it you wanted to see me about?" Leon abruptly changed the subject. His guest reacted as if he'd slapped her in the face, then attempted to cover her reaction by activating her palco to check some notes.

"I went over the data received from the expedition to the Common Border as well as some intercepted from the Ordonians. When the imperials invaded the rogue nation responsible for the attacks, they discovered all life on one of the planets had already been wiped out."

"Yes, I read a report on that. They concluded that a radiation storm hit the planet."

"It is the type of radiation that I wanted to bring to your attention. It is high-energy neutron, but on a level and frequency we've never seen before," the scientist reported, but then she hesitated.

"Go on," Leon prodded. The planet in question was close to the galactic core, a turbulent place they still knew very little about, so nothing she'd said so far had caused him any concern. However, he doubted she would have come to him in person if that's all there was to it.

"My analysis suggests an artificial origin," she finally blurted out.

"Is that even possible?"

"Yes, but it's far beyond anything we've ever been able to achieve, even in the conglomerate," the scientist responded. The room fell silent as the implications of that sunk in.

“The rogues were probably conducting an experiment and it got away from them,” the president finally concluded. He then got up and escorted her to the door while thanking her for bringing the matter to his attention.

Once back at his desk, his eyes fell to the locked drawer containing the notebook given to him by General Reno.

Was it possible?

Chapter Seventeen
Reciprocity

GCS Justice
Thursday, June 30th, 2710
4:54 P.M.

The general leaned forward in his chair as he awaited the jump to normal space, ready to get started after all the time it had taken him to gather the resources necessary to invade another Ordonian system.

In an effort to catch and keep the enemy off balance, the plan was for each of the carrier and dreadnaught groups to go in first, but each one in a different location in the system.

The destroyer groups would remain in reserve, jumping in to reinforce as needed. If they weren't needed in the initial fighting, then they would come in as a second wave to attack Athoi's defenses directly.

"One minute to destination," Navigation reported.

"Drop out of hyperspace the moment we arrive, don't wait for my order."

"Yes, sir," Helm responded.

"Sir, I still think we should stay back for a bit. We can always go in with a later wave," Captain Unther, the ship's commander, suggested.

"Negative. We go in at the head of the fleet."

The captain knew better than to argue.

"Normal space in three...two...one."

"Open fire! All batteries!"

The enemy dreadnaught in front of them already had its shields up, but those only served to protect it from standard weapons. The confederate railguns cut through the shields and hit the hull directly, inflicting heavy damage.

As per procedure, the primary targets were the shield generators, clearing the way for the rest of the Justice's considerable weaponry.

The enemy turned to face them and returned fire, but it was already too late.

Without shields and facing an enemy still at full strength, the imperials had only one choice.

The enemy weapons ceased firing, their thrusters flared with increased power and they headed straight for the Justice on a collision course.

"Target the bridge," Tyquese ordered.

There was a short hesitation from the crew, but the order was acknowledged and carried out.

It was an unofficial rule of space combat that the bridge of an enemy vessel was not to be targeted directly. Something to do with respecting an enemy's leaders, but Sam ceased to care about such things a long time ago.

The port side railgun fired, and the ray of white light streaked through space towards its target and scored a direct hit, completely destroying the enemy bridge.

With its primary control systems gone, the ship's safety protocols fired braking thrusters and brought it to a stop just a few kilometers from the bow of the Justice.

"Finish them," Sam ordered.

"They're no longer a threat," Unther protested.

"They're Imps. Of course they're still a threat."

"Yes, sir," the captain replied, then relayed the order to the crew.

The Justice fired all weapons and quickly reduced the enemy ship to little more than a cloud of dust.

The general checked his station's tactical display and saw that half of Wave Two had been called in to assist, but that wasn't unexpected. His scouts had reported the empire moving in additional defenders over the past couple weeks and he was prepared for them.

"Waves Two and Three, commence. Captain, take us to the planet."

"Confirmed."

OES Lentaise Four
7:19 P.M.

When his surprise attack on Atrias failed, Primary Canza had chosen to leave a squadron on standby near the border while he took the rest of this legion to secure the territory between that nation and the empire.

The area in question was controlled by the Amberlis Territories, so this action allowed him to continue working towards the goal of eliminating the confederacy's ability to build carriers and dreadnaughts by cutting off their supply of raw materials while also establishing a safe route for future attacks on Atrias.

Three nations stood between the Amberlis and Vehlan Territories, two of which recently joined the empire. Using this to his advantage, Canza had ordered both of them to attack while he dealt with the smaller piece of enemy territory that sat between Atrias and the third nation.

The Amberlins initially attempted to defend all three fronts, but quickly learned that to be foolish. After losing territory to the first wave of the attack, they pulled out of the space under attack by Canza to defend the bulk of their territory on the other two fronts where they were joined by confederate forces, but those reinforcements did not take action against Canza who proceeded to secure all his targets.

His immediate objectives achieved, the primary was now on his way back to Ordonian space where he would reassemble and resupply the elite legion before leading it in a new offensive against Atrias.

"Primary, we're receiving a signal from the emperor."

"I'll take it in the conference room," Canza responded.

He entered the room a moment later where he found the emperor's hologram already waiting for him.

"The system of Athoi is under attack. Take the legionnaires there immediately," Lentaise ordered without waiting for the primary to greet him.

"I increased the defenses in that system weeks ago. Are they not holding?"

"We maintain control over half the system and I have ordered up more ships, but it isn't going to be enough. The legionnaires are needed."

"It will take us days to reassemble at Athoi. If we press our attack against Atrias it may force the confederacy to withdraw to defend its shipyards."

"*No!* I will not allow another system to fall into enemy hands! You have your orders, now carry them out!"

"It will be done, Majesty," Canza replied, then sent a message to Ricine telling her to organize the legion and send it on to Athoi.

He passed through the bridge on the way to his office and gave the order to set course for Athoi, full speed.

Once in his office, he pulled up all information pertaining to the planet and its system. As it was only a low-population farming planet, he'd never been there. He wasn't about to go into a battle blind, so he would spend the next couple days studying and strategizing.

GCS Justice
Saturday, July 2nd, 2710
6:16 A.M.

"Take us into bombardment position over the capital," General Tyquese ordered.

"Sir?"

"You heard me."

"Yes, sir," Tactical responded.

"Sir, there are still enemy ships out there. We also have a 'no planetary bombardment' policy,"Captain Unther objected.

Tyquese ignored him.

"In position."

"Load nuclear warhead."

"Nukes?"

"That's what I said," Tyquese insisted.

Everyone on the bridge glanced at their comrades, but then did as they were told.

"General, may I have a word with you in the other room?" Major Briese whispered in his ear.

"I'm busy."

"With all due respect, sir, it wasn't a request," Briese insisted, and Sam whipped around to glare at him, but the major did not back down. The major's second, Captain Dodge, also took a few steps closer.

He could have them arrested for insubordination, but that would cause an awful mess if they were serious about stopping him. As Azul Guardians, they were likely capable of taking out the entire bridge crew by themselves. Even if that weren't the case, a public confrontation would undermine his authority.

"Captain Unther, you have the bridge," the general ordered, rising from his chair and storming into the conference room, Briese and Dodge close at his heels.

"What is it, Major?"

"We can't use nuclear weapons on a civilian population, sir," Briese responded while Dodge busied herself with something at the conference table.

"That's not your call to make."

"I disagree. The mass murder of civilians goes against everything I believe, and quite frankly, it goes against everything you profess to believe as well. I will not stand by and let you do this."

"Fine, you're dismissed. You can go wait in your quarters until it's over."

"No, sir, I can't."

"We're ready," Dodge cut in before Sam could respond.

"Use the table display," Briese ordered, and a moment later President Tyquese appeared as a hologram in the center of the table.

"What's going on?" he questioned. The general shot an accusatory look towards Breise, but the major simply stepped back into a corner to watch.

"Clearly, you already know what's going on," Sam scoffed.

"That's not what I meant, and you know it."

"The Imps won the last war. They never hesitated to use excessive force. If we are going to beat them this time, then we must learn from their victory."

"We will beat them without becoming them. This isn't like you. What's really going on?"

"Justice. It's long since time they received it. That is the name of this ship, after all."

"So when does it end? They bomb us...," Leon started to say, but stopped as realization overtook his features. "This is about Kate, isn't it? You want revenge."

"This is about winning the war."

"Sam, I'm not talking to you as president to general, or even soldier to soldier. I'm talking to you as brother to brother. Be honest with me," Leon insisted.

Sam grabbed the back of a chair and gripped it tight as he stared at his brother's hologram. He considered insisting this had nothing to do with their sister, but eventually released his grip as he realized such denial was pointless.

"The empire killed her. They didn't even invade the planet she was on. They simply came in, bombed the cities, then ran away. I say it's time they feel what that's like."

"I thought you blamed the union for her death."

"I do. The government failed to protect her, as was its job. They finally paid the price for their sins, but it was still the empire that pulled the trigger. They have yet to pay."

"Do you think that's what Kate would want? She died while trying to save lives. Do you really think she'd want either of us ending lives on her account?" Leon argued.

He had a point, as much as Sam hated to admit it. Their sister's mission in life was to ease suffering, to bring a little peace into a lot of war.

On a more personal note, when Sam got into fights with Leon and their parents, his anger often got the best of him and he would swear some sort of payback, but Kate wouldn't have any of that and would always find a way to calm him down. He was better than that, she would say, and he didn't have to give in to his anger.

"Goodbye, Leon," he finally said, ending the call.

He headed for the door, but was blocked by Major Briese. Neither of them said a word as they stared into each other's eyes.

Then the major nodded as if to say he understood something and stepped out of the way.

"Change of target. All military bases within range. Open fire when ready," Sam dictated on his way back to the captain's chair.

"What weapons?" Unther questioned when he saw Tactical hesitating.

He clamped his hands over the chair's armrests as if afraid he was about to fly out of it and stared at the planet displayed on the main screen.

As far as he was concerned, every last imperial deserved to die, and everyone who thought differently could jump out an airlock.

Nukes would achieve that goal quite nicely, and he imagined hundreds of mushroom clouds rising from the surface.

It was a very satisfying image.

"Conventional," he finally relented.

6:29 A.M.

A sigh of relief went through the bridge crew and they returned to their work with fervor, but Dodge couldn't help feeling some disappointment at the general's reversal. He had a point when he said the Ordonians didn't hesitate to do such things, so why should they?

"We are fighting the empire to stop such atrocities. What good does it do to win if we turn out to be no better?" Breise commented from her left.

He knew her all too well.

"The Ordonians are willing to do whatever it takes to destroy us. If we are to win, we must be willing to do the same."

"Even they know that the ends do not always justify the means. Yes, they are willing to go further than we are, but even they know there are limits. No matter how heinous they may be, their atrocities are always carried out on a tactical basis. If we strike solely for revenge, then we are actually worse."

"Good thing I prefer my revenge up close and personal anyway," she commented, refusing to admit her superior was right.

"Better thing I'm in charge and you're not," Breise shot back. She gave him an annoyed look, then the two of them returned to their posts at the general's side.

OES Lentaise Four
7:22 A.M.

Upon arriving in the Athoi system, it didn't take long for Canza to see that the space defenses were torn to shreds, and the ground defenses weren't far behind. One enemy ship was already bombing the planet, and the space defenders were unable to do anything to stop it.

"Take us straight at that dreadnaught!" Canza ordered, pointing out the ship bombing the planet.

The enemy ship ceased its bombardment, turned to face them, and accelerated away from the planet to meet them head on.

The rest of the elite legion had been spread throughout the Amberlis Territories when they received the call to defend Athoi, but given the urgency of the situation, Canza hadn't waited to finish gathering them before leaving.

As such, they were currently alone.

"Open fire the moment we're in range. All batteries."

The seconds dragged on as the two ships closed on each other, and the crew held its breath as they stared at their target on the main screen and waited for the shooting to begin.

The enemy fired first.

Two streaks of white light shot towards Canza's ship, but he did not deviate from their course.

The Lentaise Four's interceptors fired and scored direct hits.

The ship shook from two shield impacts seconds later, but their hull went undamaged. The interceptors had destroyed the solid projectile, but allowed the energy surrounding it to continue in a form their shields could block.

Now both ships fired missiles.

None made it through the interceptors.

They finally reached targeting range of the plasma cannons, and both ships opened fire with all weapons, more than any interceptor array could possibly stop.

The confederates fired their railguns again, but again they were negated without penetrating the Lentaise's shields.

"Primary! A squadron of legionnaires has just entered the system!"

"Send them to relieve the remaining garrison ships who will retreat once they are able," Canza ordered.

"Retreat?" Ricine exclaimed.

"The space defense is already lost. Nothing will be served by sacrificing more lives."

"We were ordered to defend this system!"

"We *will* defend it, but for the moment that defense has to take place on the ground to buy time for the rest of our reinforcements to arrive."

A direct hit on the hull prevented another response from Ricine, and Canza checked his command console and learned one of the enemy railgun shots had managed to get past the interceptors. He also saw that the damage was minor as their armor had taken the brunt of it.

"Take us down their starboard side, full speed. Continue firing all weapons. All infantry to transports," Canza ordered, then turned to Ricine and asked for the ETA on the rest of the legion.

"Two more squadrons will arrive in one hour, seven minutes. The rest require resupply and will not arrive for another two days at minimum," she told him.

They would never hold off the enemy space forces that long, so they had to get on the planet right away.

He looked back at the tactical display in time to see their opponent turn in their direction and dive in an attempt to get under them, but this action turned them away from the planet.

"Make for the planet. Establish orbit long enough to launch transports, then get out of here. Ricine, you're with me. Captain, you have the bridge," Canza belted out his orders, then sprung out of his chair and walked as fast as he could towards the hangar bay.

Another hull impact unsteadied him for a moment, but he recovered quickly and continued forward.

"Knight Ricine, you will take your own transport and go to our primary military base to coordinate with the planetary garrison."

"Where will you be?"

"The capital."

"Primary Canza, the garrison ships have successfully retreated," the captain updated him via his personal comm.

"Redirect all legionnaire ships to the planet. They are to off-load as many infantry personnel as possible, then you will lead them out of here. When the next two squadrons arrive, come back with them and repeat the process."

"What do we do after that?"

"Stay as close as is safe to the system and await my signal," Canza responded as he stepped onto the transport.

Athoi
Sunday, July 3rd, 2710
9:06 P.M.

The previous night and most of this day had seen constant bombardment from the confederate ships in orbit, making Canza's first priority the evacuation of the political leaders while Ricine consolidated the planetary garrison and directed the landing legionnaires. Now he stood in the capital bunker's tactical center staring at a tactical map which showed that all of their military bases were destroyed, resulting in significant casualties.

It violated his personal code of honor, but to salvage a defense contingent, Canza was forced to order all military personnel into civilian centers with the knowledge the confederacy would never bomb a civilian target.

"They finally stopped the bombardment, and will be landing ground forces soon," Canza remarked as Ricine stepped into the tactical center.

Unfortunately, their losses were still extreme. The planet's sparse population was spread out over rural areas, which slowed the evacuation considerably. Less than half of the planetary garrison was still able to fight, and the reinforcing legionnaires only brought their numbers back up to three-quarters of what they were before.

"What's your plan?" Ricine asked as she joined him in front of the tactical display.

"The garrison troops will attack the enemy wherever they land, then fall back into the forests and jungles where they will conduct a guerrilla war, forcing the confederates to use a substantial amount of personnel to hunt them down. Then you and I will take the legionnaires to the banks of the Lucion River where the remaining enemy forces will come to us."

"What's to prevent the confederates from destroying us from orbit?"

"They would have to burn down every last forest and jungle on this planet to get the garrison. As for us, any effective orbital strike would vaporize a significant portion of the river and pollute the rest. The Lucion provides water for all the farms and people in the region, so they can't afford such damage. Our remaining fighter craft will also provide air cover."

"Even if we succeed, they'll still have space control. What do you plan to do about that?"

"When we defeat their ground forces, they won't be able to launch another ground attack for several days. That will be enough time for the rest of the elite legion to counter-attack and drive them out. In the meantime, they can't destroy us from orbit without destroying the planet's value."

"So you plan to play the waiting game?"

"Exactly. They are in our territory now, where we are strongest. It is only a matter of time before we destroy them and return to our offensives."

Chapter Eighteen
Stubborn Resolve

GCS Justice
Tuesday, July 5th, 2710
10:03 A.M.

"Just as I expected," General Tyquese responded to the report of Ordonian troops massing on the west bank of the Lucion River.

"Why? There's nothing of strategic value there," Major Briese questioned.

"The location isn't important. They think the bulk of our troops are hunting down their guerrilla forces, so they're trying to draw out the rest of our divisions to destroy them and thus regain the advantage."

"They're completely exposed. We can just destroy them from orbit," Unther suggested.

"Don't you think they thought of that, Captain?" Captain Dodge remarked from her corner hiding place.

"If they had, they wouldn't have exposed themselves like this."

"You fail to give our enemy enough credit. Ordonians are not stupid," Dodge argued.

The general shot a look towards Major Briese to tell him to end the argument.

"There are two reasons we cannot fire on the enemy position from orbit. First, the Ordonians will have fighter craft standing by to intercept anything fired from orbit. The only way to counter them is to launch our own fighters, making any orbital strike impossible without killing our own people. Our numerical advantage guarantees we would eventually achieve air superiority, but the river's proximity still renders an orbital strike a lose-lose scenario," the major explained.

"Why?"

"Think of the environmental damage our weapons would do, then think of what such damage would cost us. We are here to invade this planet, not destroy it," Breise answered.

"Fortunately, I prepared for this scenario. We can defeat them with minimal damage to the planet. Captain Unther, land the Nosine divisions," Tyquese ordered.

Wednesday, July 6th, 2710
3:43 P.M.

"I've had enough of this," Canza announced, then pulled on his helmet and walked out of the command post.

"Where are you going?" Ricine called after him.

"To join the fight."

The only thing that had gone according to plan since the battle started the previous afternoon was the battle itself. Canza had miscalculated the number of enemy infantry, forcing him to fight more carefully than he'd originally planned.

He'd wanted to crush the enemy on the banks of this river, but now was barely holding his own.

He located a Razor combat jeep, ordered some nearby legionnaires to load up, then climbed into the front passenger seat. The driver and four dismount positions were quickly filled, but the last man hesitated to enter the gunner station and the primary followed his gaze to see that Knight Ricine had already taken it, recognizing her by the dull grey armor since her face was hidden by her helmet.

"You won't listen if I try to stop you, so my only option is to go along and make sure you don't get killed," she commented.

Canza chose not to reply but simply faced forward and ordered the driver to take them into the battle.

Oddly enough, he found himself somewhat comforted by her presence.

They rode in silence at the vehicle's top speed, the air whipping around them in the open cabin, but their armor shielded them where the vehicle did not.

Then the driver was forced to slow down to navigate between craters and destroyed vehicles, the results of artillery and air strikes conducted by the enemy. There were no bodies since all the casualties were carried off long ago.

The last strike was hours ago, but clouds of smoke still hung in the humid air, barely disturbed by their passing.

Stretching nearly five thousand kilometers, the Lucion River was largely surrounded by forests with some areas cleared to make way for farms, but most of the riverbanks remained wild.

In a show of brashness, Canza had chosen the one rocky region to make his stand, refusing to hide in the trees and instead challenging his enemy to come face him. This did also serve a practical purpose because the rocky ground didn't get muddy, allowing them to traverse the empty regions of the battlefield at speed.

The sounds of gunfire increased in volume, and Canza drew his pistol as he glanced up at the fighter craft of both sides dogfighting in the skies above them.

They swerved around a still smoldering Cobra tank and everyone opened fire as they suddenly found themselves in the midst of the action.

Ordonian soldiers ran from the broken front line with the confederates hot on their heels, and Canza directed his driver to take them in between the two groups.

Enemy soldiers scrambled for cover as Ricine let loose with the rapid-fire plasma turret, but few escaped the deadly accuracy of a Star Knight.

4:07 P.M.

The jeep swerved around the friendly troops while its occupants shot at the enemy as fast as they could pull their triggers, but it seemed to be doing little good. Confederate soldiers, most of them Nosines, continued to press into the imperial line and spread out through their formation.

Many of them fired on the newcomers, but the driver's maneuvering and their own reflexes kept them safe.

Movement in her periphery caught Ricine's attention and she looked up to see an enemy gunship headed for them.

She swung the turret up and opened fire at the same time the gunship fired a rocket.

Her stream of plasma bolts shot past the plane without touching it, but the rocket impacted the ground behind the jeep and kicked it into the air.

Once back on all four wheels, the driver swerved to the left, then Ricine reacquired her target and raked the gunship's underside as it flew over them.

Smoke billowed out from the fuselage, but the craft remained aloft. The damage was too severe to stay in the fight, so it turned back towards the confederate position and away from the battlefield.

Ricine returned her attention to the ground and fired again, taking out an enemy squad which had cornered several of their people.

A plasma bolt impacted the turret's blast shield, and she turned towards its source, but the one who had fired it dove behind a rock before she could return the favor.

A scream from below caught her attention, and she looked down to see one of the legionnaires holding his shoulder and grimacing in pain.

She put that of her mind and returned her attention to the battlefield just in time to see an enemy tank on their left aiming in their direction. The driver must have seen it too because he suddenly swerved to the right, but it was too late.

The tank fired, and suddenly the jeep was airborne.

Then the world went dark.

4:41 P.M.

The sounds of faint shouting and gunfire wormed its way through the fog in his head and Canza forced his eyes open to discover that he was lying facedown on the ground. He bit his tongue as unconsciousness threatened to take him again, then pressed his hands to the ground and pushed himself to his knees, then slowly rose to his feet and looked around.

The jeep he had been in lay on its side a couple meters away from him. Two of its other occupants were also on the ground nearby, but neither one moved.

The battle continued to rage around him, but for the moment, the immediate area was clear.

He stumbled over to the jeep, stopping to check on the two legionnaires on the way.

Both were dead.

Once at the jeep, he discovered Ricine hanging sideways from her harness, unconscious but alive, so he used his combat knife to cut the harness away and lowered her to the ground to check on her condition.

Her armor's medical interface indicated she didn't have any serious injuries, but there was no guaranteeing the interface and/or its sensors weren't damaged. To be sure she was okay, he'd have to check for himself.

He removed his helmet and gloves, then proceeded to remove her helmet. There were no injuries to be seen, so he felt the back of her head for any bumps or blood, but found nothing. Her breathing was also regular, and pupil response was normal.

The force of the jeep hitting the ground and the harness stopping her from flying out had knocked her out, but otherwise she was fine. If it wasn't for the armor, she'd probably be dead, the same of which could be said for him.

Secure in the knowledge that she was safe for the moment, he left her to search for the other legionnaires.

He found the driver a meter away on the other side, barely conscious and groaning. Another legionnaire stumbled up to him and reported he'd already found the final occupant dead, then helped Canza carry the driver to the other side of the jeep and lay him next to Ricine.

The primary ordered the legionnaire to tend to the driver, then went back to Ricine. Working gently, he tried to wake her up.

It took a couple attempts, but she finally opened her eyes.

"Look at me. Good, now focus. Focus on me. Good, now tell me your name," he told her.

"Wendy Ricine, Star Knight," she responded blearily.

"Where are we?"

"Athoi," she responded, then all confusion vanished from her features and she shot up into a sitting position, nearly banging heads with Canza in the process. He could tell the quick movement dizzied her, but she recovered quickly.

"What happened?" she asked.

“Our jeep was upended by a near miss from a tank shell. You were unconscious,” Canza explained.

She checked her medical status, saw she was uninjured, then jumped to her feet, but lost her balance and would have fallen if not for Canza catching her and holding on until she could find her footing.

The two of them locked eyes, and in hers he did not see a highly trained and experienced soldier, nor did he see an adversary. He saw a normal person experiencing a moment of weakness, and even detected a trace of trust towards him.

Then the moment was gone, and she pulled away. Looking anywhere but at him, she spotted her helmet on the ground and quickly picked it up and re-equipped it.

“What are we waiting for? We still have a battle to fight!” she commented while pulling her rifle from its sheath on her back.

“Are you two ready to go?” Canza asked of the two legionnaires after replacing his helmet and gloves. The driver was now fully conscious, but still sitting down.

“Yes, sir,” the one standing said, then he helped the other one up. When he had regained his balance, the driver echoed the sentiment.

Another legionnaire rounded the front of the jeep and skidded to a stop when he saw the others.

“Primary Canza?” the man questioned, breathless.

“Report in.”

“We're getting overrun, sir. The enemy brought in fresh reinforcements and routed our center.”

“Where's the rest of your squad?” Ricine asked.

“Dead.”

Two confederate soldiers walked around the front of the jeep, almost casually. Canza and Ricine reacted quickly and fired, taking them both down.

"Ricine, take the front. I'll cover the back," Canza ordered. He assigned the two legionnaires who'd been in the jeep with them to cover Ricine while he took the fresh arrival with him.

He glanced around the rear of the jeep and spotted an entire platoon of Nosine soldiers headed straight for them. Their own troops were nowhere to be seen.

The advancing enemy soldiers were clearly in no hurry, so the primary took the opportunity to check his tactical interface. In doing so, he saw that the imperial center was gone, but the flanks were still fighting.

They wouldn't hold out for much longer.

Using the interface, he ordered the flanks to fall back, then tried to establish a comlink with his command center, but soon learned his comm wasn't working.

"Anybody have a functioning comm?" he questioned. Everyone checked, but all those from the jeep responded in the negative.

"Mine's good, sir," the newest arrival reported.

"Hand it over!" Canza demanded, then took his own unit out of its slot in his helmet and tossed it to the ground.

He looked back at the advancing enemy and saw they were now too close for his comfort, so he pulled out a grenade and tossed it over the jeep.

Shouts rose from the Nosines, the grenade went off, and the imperials opened fire.

"Take over here!" Canza ordered as he took the legionnaire's comm.

He attached it to his helmet, connected with the command center, and authenticated using his personal command code.

"Primary! We've been trying to contact you!"

"Pull all units back to the transports! I am ordering a full retreat!"

"Order confirmed, but what about you!?"

"Send in response teams to get everyone off the field, then come get us!"

"Sir, we're showing significant enemy forces in your area!"

"You have your orders, Legion Commander!" Canza insisted, then cut the connection.

He took his position back from the legionnaire and looked towards the enemy to discover that they were now in cover behind rocks, in craters, or behind vehicles. It looked like there were a couple fresh bodies on the ground, but it was difficult to tell.

He saw a clear shot and fired.

Countering fire forced him to duck back, but he continued to pop out and shoot back any chance he got.

They fought like this for a couple minutes, then Canza saw the enemy tank that had destroyed their jeep coming their way once again.

"Ricine!"

"I see it!"

But there was nothing they could do about it. Their weapons were ineffective against armor, and their air support was gone.

The tank came to a stop on a mound of dirt and swung its turret around to face the wrecked jeep.

"Scatter!" Canza shouted as he bolted out of cover.

The tank fired, the jeep disappeared in a huge fireball, and the shockwave sent Canza flying into a nearby bomb crater where he rolled down the side until he came to a stop at the bottom.

"Sound off!" he shouted upon discovering he was alone. Three voices answered him, and two of the legionnaires quickly joined him.

Firing a suppression pattern behind her, Ricine jumped into the crater and slid down its side until she came to the others.

"Where's the other one?"

"He didn't make it."

Canza's blood boiled at the news, but he fought back the anger and ordered everyone who still had a grenade to throw it.

Two grenades went out, quickly followed by two explosions, then Canza climbed out of the crater and charged straight towards the Nosines in the general direction of the tank.

That thing had taken two shots at him; he was going to make sure it didn't get a third.

5:09 P.M.

When Canza ran out of the crater, Ricine followed him but stopped at the top long enough to cover the legionnaires as they also exited.

Once they were out, she ran with them into the mass of Nosine soldiers, then gripped her rifle by the barrel and swung it around to knock one of them down.

The rifle was useless at close-range, so she dropped it and pulled out her pistol and knife.

One enemy she stabbed in the waist between the torso armor and leg protection while shooting another at the same time. The Nosines were much stronger than her, so she did everything in her power to shoot them before they got too close. When one did get through, she used her agility and speed to gain the advantage by dodging their attacks and countering before they could react.

The legionnaires were less fortunate, with both out of commission minutes after the initial charge. On the other hand, Canza continued to hold his own as he made his way to the tank.

Unable to fire their main weapons without hitting their own people, two of the tank's crew climbed out to take positions on top and act as snipers. Ricine saw them and made sure to keep Nosines between her and the tank until she could get close enough to take it out.

She spotted an enemy taking aim at Canza, but she stopped him with a plasma bolt to the chest before he could pull the trigger.

She attempted to fire again, but discovered the weapon was empty and threw it at her target instead, then ran and stabbed the man under the right arm before he could recover.

Another soldier swung at her head, but she ducked out of the way, then grabbed an ankle and pulled, forcing him to the ground. He recovered quickly and aimed his rifle at her, but she knocked it aside and stabbed him in the throat.

A shout from Canza caused her to turn towards him in time to see him get body-slammed by one enemy while another covered him with a rifle.

She ran towards them, threw her knife to take out the one still standing, then tackled the other one.

Both of them rolled, but the Nosine used his superior strength to come out on top where he began choking her, but then Canza came up from behind and cut his throat.

She accepted a hand up from the primary and returned to her feet only to discover they were surrounded by at least a dozen enemy soldiers, and she was now weaponless.

"Give it up," one of the Nosines, a corporal, suggested.

"Never," Canza and Ricine spoke in unison.

"Restrain them," the corporal ordered, but his men never got the chance to obey.

The tank suddenly exploded into a ball of flame and the Nosines ducked as a wave of heat washed over them, but Canza and Ricine each crouched down and grabbed a weapon off the ground.

They opened fire as a Deathcloud rocketed past scant meters above their heads, and the Nosines shot back with one scoring a hit on Canza's shoulder.

He fell to the ground and Ricine ducked beneath another plasma bolt as she positioned herself above him and continued firing.

The Deathcloud came back and opened up with its plasma turrets, quickly killing or scattering the remaining enemy soldiers.

Ricine helped the primary up, then the two of them made their way to the descending transport while the Deathcloud kept watch from above.

"You saved my life," Canza observed.

"Twice," Ricine added.

5:52 P.M.

"What's the ETA on the rest of the legion?" Canza asked after they had evacuated the field command center and were safely away from the battle.

A medic approached him and began tending his shoulder wound while Knight Ricine activated her palco to check the latest reports.

"They finally finished resupplying in Swint and are en route. ETA is twenty hours."

"Four days ago you said it would take them two days to arrive. What took so long?" the primary questioned through gritted teeth as the medic sealed his wound.

"The Swints insisted on giving priority to their own ships, and when they did start work on ours, their inefficiency caused further delays," Ricine explained as she read from the report.

The medic finally left him alone and Canza resisted the urge to curse under his breath as he considered his remaining options.

"Send the order for them to attack the confederate blockade with the intent to open a gap long enough for us to get out. We will evade the enemy in the meantime, then escape with as many people as possible," he finally ordered.

"Do you intend to defy the emperor's order to defend this planet?" Ricine questioned.

"The confederacy will have entrenched itself by the time our reinforcements arrive, at which point it will require a full-scale invasion to retake this planet. We can't do that with the available resources."

"It is your duty to carry out the emperor's orders."

"My duty is to protect the empire and its citizens. I will not sacrifice thousands of lives and possibly victory in this war simply because I am unwilling to displease the emperor and face the resulting consequences."

"I have the authority to remove you from command and continue the fight in the emperor's name," Ricine threatened.

The primary looked at her long and hard. They had both removed their helmets shortly after boarding the transport, but she might as well still be wearing hers for what little he was able to discern from her flat expression.

"You have fought this battle with me from the start. If you believe I am misjudging the situation and that it can still be won, then do as you say," he said quietly.

She stared at him, but he did not flinch as she considered her next actions.

"No. We cannot drive the enemy from this system without depleting our national defenses to dangerous levels. Withdraw is the only option," she finally concluded.

The primary glanced around at the other soldiers, some of whom were still being treated by medics while others sat with their heads in their hands or leaning back in their seats.

Three members of the transport crew entered their section and began handing out water bottles which were gratefully accepted by the men and women fresh from the fight.

He then turned back to Ricine and said, "We have lost this battle. We will not lose the war.

Chapter Nineteen
The Will To Go On

Ordeos Prime
Saturday, July 9th, 2710
7:58 A.M.

Primary Canza and Knight Ricine marched between the fully armored and motionless knights straight to the steps of the currently empty throne dais where they each knelt with one knee on the thick red carpet.

The gunshot wound in Canza's shoulder still pained him, but it was far enough along in the healing process to require nothing more than a bandage easily concealed by his uniform. Ordonian medical science at its finest.

He focused on his breathing as he waited for the emperor to arrive, calming himself as he prepared to answer for his failure. No matter what happened, he was determined to face the consequences with dignity.

Emperor Johan finally arrived and ascended the steps to stand in front of his throne after which his personal guard took their positions around the dais.

He commanded Canza and Ricine to rise, and the primary stood perfectly straight and looked up to meet the gaze of his monarch which was locked on him with laser focus.

"You failed to defend Athoi, making it the third imperial system now under the control of anarchists. I was prepared to execute you for that," he said.

When Canza didn't respond, he looked at Ricine with the same hard expression. She faced him, but didn't meet his gaze as a gesture of respect.

"In your report, you express the belief the battle could not be won and that the primary's decision to withdraw was the only practical choice. Do you stand by that assessment?"

"Yes, Majesty."

The emperor nodded, then sat down and glared at Canza again.

"The legionnaire officers rendered the same opinion in their reports, so I have decided against removing you from your position. You will continue your efforts to destroy the confederacy, but I have ordered all your personal assets seized to be held in trust until the conclusion of this war, and I have also appointed a temporary governor at Vehla to handle your duties in that regard. You will eat, sleep, and live as a common soldier until you secure our victory or die trying."

"I understand, and I will not rest until all our enemies are defeated."

"Begin by recalling all remaining occupation forces from the Vehlan territories and turning responsibility for their defense over to the local legions. That will give Secondary Zenzal enough units to repel the invaders while you focus on our offensives."

"Three of the Vehlan planets remain in open revolt, Highness."

"The local forces can take over those counter-insurgencies as well. They are imperial military now and it's time we begin using them. I also want you to send extraction teams to pull out the last of our troops from the Merchant's Interest. There is nothing left to be gained by leaving them there, but we can put them to use elsewhere."

"I agree. Is there anything more, Majesty?"

"You are dismissed. Knight Ricine, stay. I have more to discuss with you," Lentaise said.

The primary bowed and turned to leave, but the emperor had one last thing to say.

"Every last vestige of my patience will disappear should you fail me again, no matter the reasons or what anyone else has to say on your behalf."

8:21 A.M.

"As the elite legion's executive officer, it is your responsibility to ensure their battle-readiness. Why were they unavailable for so long?" Johan Lentaise questioned Knight Ricine.

"I ordered them to resupply at a Swint outpost en route to Athoi, but they encountered multiple delays which prevented them from reaching the battle in time to render assistance. My mistake was in trusting the Swints, and I recommend it become standard procedure for our units to be supplied exclusively by Ordonian outposts."

"The nation of Swint agreed to become part of the empire, so they are Ordonians now. Are you saying we can't trust them?"

"It did take them twice as long to resupply our ships as it should have. Is it possible they are secretly working with the confederacy but joined with us so they could act as spies and saboteurs?" Ricine suggested.

That possibility hadn't occurred to Johan. It was unusual for any nation to choose to give up its sovereignty to be absorbed by another. Not even those that had formed the Vehlan Union had done that, with the individual governments having eroded away over time.

Was it possible the inefficiency of the Swints was not simply that which they had come to expect from all foreigners but rather a deliberate ploy to hinder the war effort?

"I will have Master Knight Penavel find out if this is the case, and we will construct our own facilities within Swint and Jinara to service our forces," he finally decreed, then told Ricine she could leave.

OES Lentaise Four
9:32 A.M.

"Not long after we first met, you asked me why I would vouch for you in front of the emperor. I now find myself wondering the same thing," Canza commented as he joined Ricine in the ship's tactical room.

"I merely told the truth," Ricine responded without looking away from her terminal.

"You merely told the truth to an angry emperor who likely saw things differently. He could have punished you for supporting me."

"It is my honor-bound duty to tell the truth, regardless of the consequences."

"Most people care more about self-preservation than honor."

"It doesn't matter to me what most people would do. What matters to me is doing the right thing."

"That's why I wanted to keep you around," Canza revealed, and Ricine finally looked at him with narrowed eyes.

"What do you mean?" she asked.

"You're not like most people."

Her only response was to look back at the terminal and Canza followed her gaze to see the casualty lists from Athoi displayed on the monitor.

"What's the final tally?" he asked, but found himself wishing they could continue talking about each other.

"22,382 dead, 25,457 wounded, 432 missing," Ricine listed off.

"That brings us to over forty-thousand legionnaires dead since the beginning of the war."

"The biggest losses have been to the Nosines."

"Losing personnel is bad enough, but losing them to slaves is insulting. If they'd fought like this for the first emperor, then they never would have become slaves in the first place."

"It's truly ironic that they fight for someone to free themselves from an enslavement that's the result of their refusal to fight for someone," Ricine observed, and Canza let out a short laugh before he caught himself and cleared his throat.

"Slaves or not, they are causing us losses we cannot afford. The average soldier can be replaced relatively easily. When a legionnaire dies, there is no replacement, and there are only sixty-thousand left. We need to start training more."

"That's something the emperor needs to approve."

"There's no reason he wouldn't. The legionnaires have more than proven themselves."

"There is still opposition from some in the military and the government to the idea of an elite legion trained from near-birth. They will say the legionnaires could still pose a threat," Ricine pointed out.

"All the other programs failed long before now. The emperor knows that, and he can see how well the legion has performed. He can easily silence any doubters."

"What about the defeat on Athoi?"

"The blame for that is mine, not the legion's. There's also the fact the losses would have been far more severe with any other legion," Canza argued.

Several seconds passed as Ricine simply stared at the casualty list still displayed before her, no doubt calculating the risks and numbers in her head.

"A new class of legionnaires is possible, but not one every year. There's no possible way to support that many alongside the regular military."

"What do you suggest?"

"A new class every ten years," she answered.

Now it was the primary's turn to think things over.

Unlike the average soldier, the legionnaires were in the military for life. If a new class graduated every year, they would eventually outnumber the regular military leading to fewer and fewer soldiers returning home to take civilian jobs and thus support the economy.

It might be possible for them to have the entire military as elite legionnaires once all of humanity was united under the Ordonian banner. Many of those who were now their enemies might never be trusted enough to serve, so those citizens would provide the civilian workforce.

But for now, Ricine was right.

"Agreed. Contact the emperor and start making the arrangements." he ordered, and Ricine left the room to compose the message in private.

Now that he was alone, Canza found himself unable to focus on his work, but found himself dwelling on recent events instead.

The emperor's punishment, a harsh one for most people, hardly affected him at all. He already spent most of his time on the job, almost never going to his house or spending his money. His work meant far more to him than any of those things.

It was the failures themselves that haunted him. Until the battle in the Merchant's Interest, he'd never failed at anything. Now, he'd failed twice.

He knew that his tactics were perfect, their execution flawless. Those under his command always performed admirably, and their equipment was the best to be had.

The possibility occurred to him that someone else was simply better, but he immediately dismissed the thought as absurd.

He was missing something, but had no idea what it could be.

For the first time in his life, fear crept into his heart as he realized there existed the possibility of the empire losing this war. If *he* couldn't figure this out, who could?

Chapter Twenty
A Doom Appears

GCS Tyranny's End
Monday, August 29th, 2710
8:19 A.M.

The tactical map displayed on the desk hadn't changed over the last two hours, but President Tyquese still couldn't decide where he wanted to take the fleet now orbiting Asilon IV.

"The war continues to drag on, but all sources are hopeful it will resolve itself soon in victory for the confederacy," the Merchant news anchor said on the video feed in the desk's upper left corner.

"Keep dreaming," Leon muttered as he tapped the video to turn it off.

Almost two months ago, Sam had managed to capture the Ordonian system of Athoi, but had made no further progress since he needed all his resources to fend off the constant enemy counterattacks.

Meanwhile, an Ordonian fleet was still sitting on the border of Atrias. They'd attacked twice, but were repelled both times, and Leon had mandated that one out of every two new dreadnaughts be added to the defense. Now it appeared the Ordonians were biding their time, waiting for the confederate defenses to expose a weakness.

Small skirmishes continued to pop up all over, but they were of little consequence. Some of them were former pirates conducting raids, but most of them were nothing more than the two sides unexpectedly running into each other and firing a few shots.

The war was frozen. Neither side could make a move without sacrificing something important.

The only way the confederacy would have enough ships to assault the increased Ordonian defenses would be to pull them from Atrias, but doing so meant sacrificing it to the enemy.

Meanwhile, a fresh offensive from the empire would expose its inner territories to attack.

With no options available to him using standard tactics, Leon had decided it was necessary to use the alien technology on Asilon IV. They'd avoided using it except when absolutely necessary for fear the empire would figure out they had it.

The fleet he'd be using in this attack was ready to go, but Leon still wasn't convinced about what would be the best target.

He wanted to strike within the empire, but knew the Ordonians would wonder how they got in and out without passing the border sensor nets and he couldn't take the risk the resulting investigation would lead them to Asilon IV.

His instincts told him to attack the enemy invaders in the Amberlis Territories to take the pressure off his allies, but he could accomplish that without using the alien technology and it wouldn't be much help in the long-run.

An option that provided the best of both worlds was to attack either the nation of Swint or that of Jinara. It would not be obvious how they had gotten in, and it would take some pressure off the Amberlins.

It wasn't ideal, but it was the logical choice, so he picked a target in Jinara and walked out onto the bridge to give the order, but was interrupted by Communications.

"We're receiving a distress call from the Brazark Federation, sir."

"From the federation itself; not the border?" Leon questioned as he sat in the captain's chair.

"Affirmative."

"Odd that they would send it so far. What's it say?"

"They report a breach in the Common Border and that they are under heavy attack. They are calling for all possible aid."

"More rogues?"

"No, sir, it doesn't sound like it. The report states the federation's defenses are ineffective."

He was relatively unconcerned before, but the idea of the Brazark defenses being ineffective shot through Leon like a lightning bolt.

With all known weapon technologies, a nation's defenses should be at least moderately effective. For them to be totally ineffective required something previously unknown, which indicated a threat not just for the nations on the border, but for those in the core as well.

"Condition Red! Signal the planet to send us to the Brazark Federation immediately!" he snapped out his orders.

The ship switched into battle mode, there was a flash, and the planet disappeared from the main screen to be replaced by a field of stars.

A journey normally requiring weeks to make was over in a matter of seconds, but even so, they were too late.

The president looked at the surrounding space via both the main screen and his command console, but saw only debris.

The battle was already over.

"Large fleet detected at edge of system. Unknown affiliation."

"Let me see."

The view on the main screen switched to show the fleet in question, then magnified for a better look, and Leon slowly rose from his seat as he took it in.

It was the largest fleet he had ever seen! It could easily match the entire space based military of either the confederacy or the empire!

As he watched, a quarter of the fleet broke off from the main body and headed on an intercept course towards the confederates. When this happened, it became clear that this fleet was divided into fours, with each division sporting its own unique architectural style, none of which were familiar.

There were only two types of ships in the section moving to intercept them, the smaller of which were spherical while the larger appeared to be stepped domes.

"Hail them," Tyquese ordered. The hail was accepted, and half the main screen was given over to show his counterpart which elicited gasps from everyone on the bridge.

The person that appeared on the screen was not human, but looked like a giant insect of some kind. The closest comparison the president could make was to a praying mantis, except its arms, hands, and legs were more humanoid.

"Who are you and why have you attacked this nation?" Tyquese demanded.

"You have forgotten us, but we have not forgotten you. We have come to reclaim that which is ours," the alien hissed back at him in the same language.

"I represent a coalition of several nations. If you send a delegation to meet with us, perhaps we can come to terms."

"There will be *no* terms! All humans will die!"

"This need not escalate further," Leon started to argue, but the alien cut the connection.

"Hostile ships still on approach!"

"We can't fight that many. Contact Asilon IV and have them teleport us back," Leon ordered.

As soon as they were back at the planet, he contacted the facility's Vaton director and asked how long it would take to evacuate the facility while taking as much of its technology as possible with them.

"At least several weeks," the director responded, a note of confusion in his voice.

"I'm not talking about tearing down the entire facility and taking it with us! Give me the bare minimum!"

"In an emergency situation, I'd say a day."

"Good. Get started right away," Leon ordered, then added, "And this *is* an emergency situation."

The call ended, and Leon ordered a new one to Sam.

"I'm still not convinced what I saw was real, but if it was, won't we be needing this facility if we are to stand a chance?" the ship's captain, Yula Escamilla, questioned.

"Those aliens saw us use the technology, and odds are they know more about it than we do. They are probably already on their way," Leon responded.

"Even so, it will take weeks for them to get here. Shouldn't we use that time to dismantle and take with us as much of the technology as possible?"

"You saw those ships and what they did to the Brazarks. There's no way to know how much faster they are than our own ships. We take what we can, as fast as we can." Leon responded, his tone signaling the end of the conversation.

"What's going on?" Sam greeted crankily after the connection was made.

"We have a much bigger problem than the empire on our hands."

GCS Tyranny's End
Tuesday, August 30th, 2710
4:27 A.M.

"Can you tell what it is?" Leon asked when Tactical reported something was coming towards them.

He'd spent the entire previous day and night supervising the evacuation of Asilon and conferencing with Sam, but any fatigue he was feeling disappeared as he felt his heartrate shoot up from the adrenaline now flooding his system.

"Negative. I've never seen anything like it."

"Condition Red! How long until they arrive?"

"Now," Tactical responded, and several hundred ships suddenly appeared all around them.

"Get everyone off the planet immediately! Leave everything that isn't already loaded up and get them out of there!" Leon ordered.

An alien squadron broke off from the main fleet and headed for the humans while the rest of their ships took up blockade positions.

"Fire the moment they are in range, don't wait for my command!"

"They've opened fire!" Tactical shouted the same moment everyone else saw it on the main screen.

A bright red beam shot out from one of the alien ships and impacted a Vehlan destroyer. There was a flash of light and several small explosions on the ship's hull which indicated shield collapse.

The aliens fired three more shots. One struck the bow, the second hit center, and the last sliced through the stern.

Four shots, and one of their most powerful ships was gone before it could even bring its own weapons into range.

"We can't stand against that!"

"We have to get out of here!"

"No! We still have a job to do! Full speed ahead!"

The confederates charged towards their foe, but within seconds another two ships were gone.

"Take evasive action! Don't rely on your defenses!" Leon called out.

Everyone complied, and the next shot missed.

Now within range, the confederates opened up with everything they had to score several direct hits, but there appeared to be no effect on the aliens.

"We have to concentrate our firepower! All ships, fire on this target!" Leon ordered as he selected a target using his command interface.

All those in the vicinity surrounded the enemy ship and fired all weapons, finally causing some damage.

"The last of the evac shuttles are launching now!"

"Enemy units moving to intercept!"

"Let's get their attention. All ships link your weapons' systems with Tyranny's End. Tactical, program all ships to fire when you do."

"It will take a few seconds!" Tactical responded, and Leon nodded his affirmation.

The confederate ships ceased firing as the systems were linked and programmed, but they continued flying in all directions, desperately trying to avoid the powerful alien weapons.

Leon could do nothing but watch and sweat while Tactical worked.

"You said a *few* seconds!" he shouted upon seeing another ship explode.

"Ready, sir!"

"Fire all batteries!"

Each of the dreadnaught's weapons fired, excluding its nuclear launcher, and the others did the same.

Receiving hundreds of hits at once proved too much for the target, and its shields collapsed. Two more volleys, and it was destroyed.

"It worked!"

The alien ships that had been going after the evac shuttles turned around to come back at the warships, and several more broke off from the main fleet to do the same.

The Tyranny's End received a direct hit and Leon gripped his chair tight as the ship shook from the impact.

"First shield layer gone!"

"Evac shuttles away! Ground facility self-destruct detonated!"

"All ships, retreat!"

"There's too many of them, sir! We can't get to clear space!"

"Then don't! Everybody jump where you are!"

Two more ships were destroyed, but the rest managed to make it into hyperspace.

"Are they following?"

"Negative, sir."

"They must not feel we're worth the effort. Helm, get us out of here before they change their minds."

Chapter Twenty-One
New Priorities

Ordeos Prime
Wednesday, August 31st, 2710
1:07 P.M.

The two sides are too evenly matched. The only way to break this stalemate is to sacrifice something, but what can we afford to lose in exchange for taking something more valuable away from the enemy? Canza considered as he stared at the main screen in the palace's tactical center.

"Primary Canza! Confederate forces have evacuated the Athoi system!"

"What!" Canza exclaimed, then walked over to the relevant station to see for himself.

"The system reported in a few minutes ago to report the enemy's absence and request new defense units," the operator explained.

"Raxin is reporting the same thing, sir," another operator reported.

"As is Erebus, sir!"

"Tell Secondary Zenzal to get all available units into those systems!" Canza ordered before returning to the central station.

"Sir, Amberlin forces have ceased their campaign to retake their territory!"

"At least two raids against our supply lines were pulled back before they could finish!"

"Nosine rebels have withdrawn from all active battles!"

"Are they preparing to surrender?" someone speculated.

"No. Something else is going on here," Canza responded.

He opened the console's communications interface and keyed in the code that granted him instant access to the emperor.

"What's going on?" Lentaise questioned.

"The confederate forces in our territory have retreated, and all others have withdrawn from battle. Something has spooked them, and it isn't us. I recommend putting all our forces on standby until we learn more."

"Do it. I'm on my way," Lentaise agreed.

The room burst into a flurry of activity as dozens of operators relayed the standby order to the hundreds of imperial holdings.

One by one, the lights on the galactic map switched from green or red active indicators to yellow standby status. As he watched, the primary saw it as the galaxy taking a deep breath, then holding it.

Unknown Location
Thursday, September 1st, 2710
9:09 A.M.

The admiral stood on the station's observation deck looking out at the stars, his white uniform reflecting back at him. After centuries of isolation, it would soon be time for his people to head back out towards those stars.

The aliens had forgotten about them, and the rest of humanity considered them a myth. Their grand return would ensure they were never forgotten about again.

His dress shoes clicking on the tiles below him, a vice-admiral walked up to join him.

"It's started."

"I know."

If you enjoyed *Total War,* continue the story in *Brink of Extinction!*

Appendix A
Characters

Leon Tyquese (President)

Age: 38
Gender: Male
Ethnicity: Vehlan
Hair Color/Style: Brown/Military Cut
Eye Color: Grey
Height: 5', 7"
Build: Lean, Athletic

Leon was born on the planet Vehla, homeworld of a nation that had been at war for over seventy years. As soon as he was old enough to understand, he embraced the patriotism of his people and dedicated his life to their cause.

He joined the Vehlan Union infantry as a commissioned officer once he was of age, and served with excellence, his stubborn resolve inspiring those around him to fight harder while his insightful tactics often turned certain defeat into victory. This pattern of service eventually earned him a promotion to the staff of General Reno, commander-in-chief of the union military.

Military service was still voluntary at this time, but preparation programs for children were prevalent with the expectation that nearly everyone would end up choosing to serve.

As long as he remains alive, Leon Tyquese will continue to fight tyranny no matter the odds.

Sam Tyquese (General)

Pirate Designation: Red Sam
Age: 35
Gender: Male
Ethnicity: Vehlan
Hair Color/Style: Black/Short
Eye Color: Grey
Height: 5', 6"
Build: Thick, Muscular

The world that Sam was born into was one that had been at war for nearly eighty years. Despite the zealous patriotism that permeated his culture, he never wanted anything to do with that war and wished only to live his own life doing what he loved. This didn't sit well with his parents or older brother Leon, the latter of which constantly pressured him into attending the military preparation programs for children.

When it came time to enlist, he reluctantly joined the Vehlan Union fleet. His performance was average in that he properly performed any task assigned to him, but he never did anything more than was required of him.

A confrontation with a superior officer led to his desertion in no longer caring what anyone else thought. Now a fugitive with no place to go, he made his way to the pirate planet where he joined the red faction.

In fighting to survive, he learned how to thrive.

Max Canza (Primary)

Age: 40
Gender: Male
Ethnicity: Ordonian
Hair Color/Style: Bronze/Military Cut
Eye Color: Dark Blue
Height: 6', 3"
Build: Medium, Athletic

As the only child of moderately wealthy parents in the Ordeon Empire, Max was raised to be their greatest achievement in life. They enrolled him in advanced schooling and physical training with the requirement he excel at every task given to him. He embraced this life, managing to exceed everyone's expectations and even seeking out new challenges on his own.

Since he was committed to a lifelong military career, Max chose to complete his education before joining. His pattern of excellence continued in both school and as a military officer. When he successfully completed a seemingly impossible mission, he came to the attention of the emperor himself who then assigned him command of the final invasion of their enemy's homeworld.

Now Max is right where he needs to be to finally crush his people's worst enemy and open the way to achieving their destiny.

Helen Dodge (Captain)

Nickname: Dodger
Age: 32
Gender: Female
Ethnicity: Swarnlian (Vehlan Province)
Hair Color/Style: Dark Red/Military Cut
Eye Color: Dark Green
Height: 5', 9"
Build: Medium, Athletic

A rebel from the moment she was born, Helen has always clashed with the people around her, including her own family with her mother being the only one to show any real patience with her. As a child she would often go off alone into town or the woods around her home to explore, further developing her independent personality and learning self-reliance to go with it.

A strong desire to stand with her people against the Ordeon Empire did nothing to curb her rebellious nature and new conflicts arose after joining the officer's academy. This is until Peter Briese, a visiting special forces operative, saw something in her and got her transferred to Azul Guardian training.

Upon successful completion of the course, she returned to the academy and finished her schooling with a minimum of incidents, after which her mentor added her to his team. Her companions know not to get on her bad side, but they also recognize no one is more loyal or better to have with them in a fight.

Wendy Ricine (Knight)

Age: 38
Gender: Female
Ethnicity: Ordonian
Hair Color/Style: Medium Blonde/Military Cut
Eye Color: Bright Green
Height: 5', 9"
Build: Lean, Athletic

The first part of Wendy's life was rather unremarkable. Every task required of her she did quite well, but she never went above and beyond or sought anything out on her own.

When she joined the Ordonian infantry, she did so without any purpose in her life, once again only doing what was expected of her. Then she saw the suffering caused by war as well as crime and poverty from which she had largely been sheltered as an imperial citizen, finally igniting a passion within her.

An act of heroism earned her a recommendation from her superior officer to join the Star Knights, the emperor's personal guard and most elite warriors in the empire. Now she is in the place where she can do the most good, and she won't let anyone stand in her way.

Appendix B Factions

Main Factions

Ordeon Empire

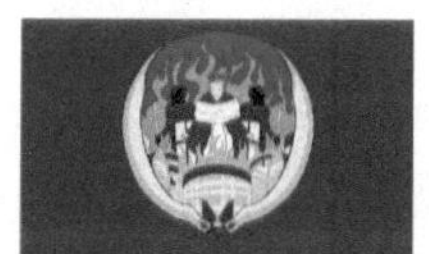

Type of Government: Imperial Monarchy
Head of State: Emperor
Economy: Imperialist/Capitalist
Homeworld: Ordeos
Capital City: Ordeos Prime
Controlled Systems: 21 Provinces

The Ordeon Empire has been on a quest of total domination since its inception, held in check only by the Vehlan Union. Their reasons for this quest have varied throughout history, but presently imperial citizens honestly believe the empire is humanity's only hope for a brighter future. If others refuse to acknowledge this fact, then they are holding the human race back and must be eliminated.

At least six years of military service is required of all citizens. The youngest age they can join is eighteen, but they are given the choice of joining right away or completing their schooling before joining. This system ensures the empire's military maintains the maximum possible strength at all times.

Vehlan Union (Destroyed)

Type of Government: Democratic Republic
Head of State: Chancellor
Economy: Capitalist
Homeworld: Vehla
Capital City: United
Controlled Systems: 17

Originally formed out of several nations for the purpose of mutual defense and easier trade, the Vehlan Union was originally intended to remain a group of sovereign nations working together, but eventually became a single nation.

The nation has always sought to maintain individual liberty for all people, even non-citizens, which resulted in them fighting several wars with the Ordeon Empire to halt its campaigns of conquest.

Military service was optional until the last few years of the Hundred Years War, but strong patriotism moved most citizens to join despite not being required to do so.

Galactic Confederacy

Type of Government: Confederate
Head of State: President
Economy: Tax-Based
Homeworld: New Hope
Capital City: Undecided
Controlled Systems: 1 (Owned solely by the confederate government and not by a member nation)

Pirates and union soldiers formed the Pirate League, which then grew into the Galactic Confederacy when four sovereign nations were convinced to join. Those nations were the Merchant's Interest, Vaton Conglomerate, Amberlis Territories, and Atrias. All four of these nations had once belonged to the Vehlan Union but had seceded and become independent entities for various reasons.

The pirates and union remnants became the military and political forces of the confederacy while member nations contribute to both as they see fit.

Appendix C Glossary of Terms

Ship Tags

(The acronym before a ship's name designating its affiliation.)

G.C.S. - Galactic Confederacy Ship
O.E.S. - Ordeon Empire Ship
R.P.S. - Red Pirate Ship
V.U.S. - Vehlan Union Ship

Bridge Stations

In the interest of saving time, the operator of each bridge station is referred to by the name of that station as if it were their own name. This way a commanding officer only has to call out for the station he/she wants, and not for the person operating the station at that particular moment. Stations on larger ships are operated by more than one officer, so the senior officer is the one who will respond to orders or requests for information.

On smaller ships, some of these stations are combined, but following is a list of each one as a separate entity.

Helm - The pilot's station responsible for the flight operations of the craft. Normally crewed by a single operator.

Navigation - This station controls the sensors which monitor navigational hazards around the ship such as asteroids and gravity wells and also contains detailed charts for plotting courses through hyperspace. It is usually crewed by one or two operators or is combined with the helm station.

Tactical - The position overseeing a vessel's combat systems including threat detection and targeting sensors, shield operation, and weapons. Normally crewed by one personnel but can have up to five, with the additional officers adding the ability to monitor other ships in a formation.

Systems - This station is responsible for overseeing all ship functions which do not fall under a specialized category, such as life support and cargo/personnel transfers. Operated by between three to seven crew.

Communications - The station responsible for all internal and external communications aboard ship. Up to four personnel can be assigned here, but on smaller ships it is combined with the tactical station.

Threat Conditions

Each national military operates under a common set of threat conditions. It's believed that this system was put in place when the human race was unified under one banner, but there is no evidence to support this fact.

Condition Yellow - No threat detected. Shields at minimum. Weapons deactivated. Crew maintains alertness, watching at all times for any possible threats. Standard operating condition for every military vessel.

Condition Orange - Possible threat detected. Shields at maximum. Weapons placed in standby. On-duty crew called to battle stations.

Condition Red - Threat confirmed. Shields at maximum. Weapons activated. Fighters launched. All crew to battle stations. Power diverted to combat systems.

Damage Levels

When ships are damaged during the course of a battle, commanding officers need to instantly know the extent of the damage. Toward that end, a system is in place that conveys that information with one or two words.

Minor - Shields damaged. Possible damage to hull. No systems affected.

Moderate - Shields heavily damaged, possibly collapsed. Damage to the hull. Some systems are damaged and/or disabled.

Heavy - Shields off-line. Significant damage to hull, with possible breaches. Several systems are damaged, disabled, or destroyed. Ship is still battle capable.

Severe - All battle systems disabled or destroyed. Significant damage to hull. Ship may still be capable of flight, or is completely disabled.

Destroyed - The ship is damaged beyond hope of repair but parts and materials may still be salvageable.

Miscellaneous Terms

Imp - A slang term used by Vehlans to denote people of Ordonian origin. It is short for "Imperial," but is also a reference to the mythological creature as a way to say the empire and its citizens are evil.

Nihl - A slang term used by Ordonians for people from the Vehlan Union. It comes from the word "Nihilist" and is meant to say that Vehlans have no respect for law and order. A secondary meaning references the philosophical ideas about nothingness which is their way of saying the Vehlans are nothing compared to them.

Palco - Short for palm-computer, this is a microcomputer embedded in the palm of the hand which is accessed via a holographic interface activated by a specific muscle movement which is chosen by the user. It is also the name of the first commercial distributor of the product, but the term is now used in reference to all such devices regardless of the brand.

Acknowledgements

Thank you to my dad for his continued support and encouragement on this never-ending journey of mine.

Special thanks to artist Calley Dunnihoo who created the first cover and has stuck with me on this journey from the first edition to the current revision.

And to all my friends who tolerate my rambling on about non-existent worlds and my constant requests for feedback.

About the author

An active imagination has been one of Dodge's defining attributes for as long as he can remember, with its creations often seeming more real to him than the world in which he lived. Upon discovering a talent and affinity for the written word, he began writing stories for fun at first, then eventually decided to make it more than a hobby. This has taught him to control his wandering mind while also providing an escape for him and others.

Born in northern Illinois, his family moved to southern Missouri shortly afterward where he currently lives with his two cats Merry and Pippin who provide comfort and drive him crazy multiple times a day. He rides a motorcycle, exercises regularly, and trains in Brazilian Jiu-Jitsu when possible.

Also by Dodge Merrin

Follow me on Amazon!

Embers of Hope Science Fiction Miniseries

<u>Triumphant Empire</u>

Available through Amazon & KU.

Revolution

Available through Amazon.

Total War

Available through Amazon.

Brink of Extinction

Available through Amazon.

See Also

Humble Glory

Available through Amazon & KU.

www.ingramcontent.com/pod-product-compliance
Lightning Source LLC
LaVergne TN
LVHW090600110826
845146LV00001B/200